He's Growing

Zach Kauffman

He's Growing

A novel

Many thanks to Bradley, Esther and Stefanie

First paperback edition
ISBN: 9783982255606 (paperback)
ISBN: 9783982255613 (ebook)

121 23 483 42 120 39 9 294 60 255 270 264 15 196 133 500 2 476 260 99 280

Table of Contents

This book is dedicated to
Rosa Sierra

1 – Copper fleece

The texture of his fur was wondrous. It was a reflection of his exceptionality – cunning and multilayered. Usually it gave him those mischievous traits that people liked so much. In most cases, he got what he wanted because anyone who saw, touched or smelled him could not resist his allure.

The soft hair stood up and formed an especially fluffy carpet over his skin. It accentuated his chubby face, his big button eyes and short ears. With a cunning smile on his face, he appeared mischievous and attentive. People seemed to trust his easygoing nature. They loved it when he darted towards them with large, elegant steps, only to turn away right in front of their shin, and wrap his head and body around their legs. His fur left a scent on their clothes with which he marked possible backers.

For people whose hearts he wanted to win over, he jumped onto their backs from behind as soon as they bent down to pet him. From there, he went to the shoulder, to rub his nose against the person petting him. They loved him for that, and they sometimes had treats for him, in addition to stroking him.

No one could suspect him of ill intentions. Even critical contemporaries and dog lovers trusted him and questioned what they knew about cats at the sight of him. If cats were considered treacherous and disloyal a moment ago, he suddenly reversed those certainties. His cuddly fluff convinced many a doubter.

His exquisite fur was dominated by various shades of orange. A copper shimmer gave him something sublime. A fine, reddish stripe ran along the shining white chest.

However, appearances could be deceiving. His true mood could not be reliably read from his cute look and cuddly shape. He was able to consciously control his appearance and used this ability to manipulate humans and animals, friends and foes. Sometimes he – like other cats – puffed up his fur to increase his profile and feign size that was not there. But sometimes he also puffed up his fur to look cuddly, friendly and gentle. Then, with his rounded form he almost appeared trusting, while he in truth he was calculating and dangerous.

Sometimes, he changed his shape when his mood darkened. His fur lost its shimmer, became dull and dark. He compressed it, appearing angular and agile. The sleek fur emphasized his muscles. His sharp claws were free. His fur was so taut that it clung to his body like a leather sheath, giving him protection from his adversaries' teeth and paw blows. Then a biting smell spread, numbing all senses. His eyelids closed to slits. The upright pupils were so narrow that their black could only be recognized as a thin line. His posture was crouched and full of tension, demonstrating his immediate readiness to strike first or defend himself. He had no need for any optical illusion, like the flaring of the fur, in order to appear threatening to other animals. He showed himself as he was: threatening.

He hardly lacked self-confidence, especially since he always looked dazzling and extremely well-groomed. His fur repelled all kinds of dirt, because his hair had a surface structure like lotus blossoms, to which nothing stuck. He was never ridiculed because of a dirty or soaked coat. Not even the filth of days long past, which had been rotting in some dark corner, was able to stick to him for more than a brief moment. And if someone else's spit hit him, he only had to shake briefly and was instantly clean again. It was amazing how little of even the most disgusting dirty work remained as a blemish on his fur. Everything simply rolled off him.

And although it could not matter to him, everyone who tried to sully him had to count on crude resistance. If someone threw dirt at him, his fur became bristly and hard like that of a wild boar. If he was approached, he could suddenly discard his usual apathy. Smaller opponents then inevitably fell victim to him. He pursued them relentlessly and punished them cruelly. Only those who played dead or submitted unconditionally got off. Then, he loosened the claw-grip of his front-paws and refrained from making the opponent the garrote with powerful pushes of his claw-reinforced hind legs. Usually, however, he knew no bounds when it came to silencing his opponents. Only rarely did he reveal himself to be benevolent.

It gave him great pleasure to be condescending. Since he had only little regard left for rodents or weaklings of the like, these had to endure the most. They were equally blinded and out-shined by the brightness of his mane what showed them their inferiority with exceeding clarity. He loved his copper shine and knew nothing better than to look at it in the mirror of every water surface.

2 – Prowl

The colors of his fur merged with the red and brown leaves that covered the ground everywhere. The autumn foliage allowed him to hide his movements. When he slept or, as so often, indulged in idleness, he was almost invisible. He loved the sight of the falling leaves and the way they performed dances, carried by the breeze. Beautiful like the fragments of a spinning kaleidoscope when a vortex of air hit them once again, before they finally piled up into colorful drifts. The loud rustling of dry mounds of leaves in the wind covered all the sounds of the forest. Only the wind itself was sometimes louder.

Autumn was impetuous, beautiful and overflowing with food. A cornucopia was poured out over the tomcat. Whenever he felt hungry, he would spontaneously go hunting and was rewarded with a lavish yield, because all the animals of the forest were on their way to bulk up for the cold season. Nature offered more food than he could eat.

For weeks, he was out and about, eating when he was hungry and sleeping when he was tired. He often had the opportunity to lounge around and enjoy the day. Usually, he looked for a sheltered spot with a good view. There he would tread a few times in one place to make a soft nest of grass and leaves. Before lying down, he turned around in circles once or twice to find a comfortable resting position. Then, he could spend hours with nothing doing.

If he felt like it, he continued his expedition to find a new place where it was even nicer than the previous one. It was so beautiful that he wished this season would never pass. He would have liked to hold on to autumn forever.

Little by little, however, winter inevitably overtook the landscape. Since the first snowfall, it was uncomfortable and bare in the forest. The comfort of soft deciduous mountains and full menu options gave way to the emptiness of the omnipresent white. Corners and edges disappeared under a frosty sheet. A shapeless evenness had overlaid the autumnal disorder. He was robbed of his camouflage and his orange coat stood out conspicuously from the surroundings. Hardly any color, hardly any sound broke through the monotony of winter. A soft murmur sounded with every step in the snow and was swallowed again immediately. The winter forest was quiet. Only the warning calls of other animals could be heard, when they saw him from far away.

His favorite foods turned tail and fled or from the get-go completely remained in their burrows, nests and dwellings. What is more, their entrances could hardly be discovered in the snow. The fact that plants and nuts were also difficult to find in winter hardly bothered him, since he preferred to leave such nibbles to more insignificant creatures. His diet was only supplemented by vegan food in the form of stowaways from the stomachs of his victims. Searching for food was now difficult, and so the hunger plagued him more and more often.

He wanted to finally have fresh meat again. And since he found it appropriate that his food was brought to him, it was time to find a human family to move in with. After weeks of wandering through an increasingly inhospitable landscape, he would be warmed and cared for there. He would make himself comfortable in cozy rooms. Perhaps his cuddly fur and cute eyes helped him find bona fide bipeds whose caring hands would try to save a helpless kitten from the cold, not realizing his calculating intentions.

However, it was not easy finding a suitable family to spend the winter with. He had come too far off the beaten path on his meanderings. Monotony repressed all sense of time. He spent another few days in this icy wasteland, and he was neither able to reliably measure the duration nor direction of his prowling. But the column of smoke from a chimney suddenly announced the arrival of civilization.

There it lay, the village that would soon become his new home. Where the foothills of a wooded hilly landscape merged into the sheer endless expanse of the plain, lay the small pile of houses. The top of a church tower loomed between the roofs. Beyond that, the fields reached as far as the eyes could see. It seemed to be a village like any other. So the cat was sure to find people here who would take him in. Because he had often come on his foray through similar villages where nice people would give a fluffy little fellow like him a delicious bowl without ever making demands or prescribing anything. He had always been able to do what he wanted and never had to follow rules. He ate his fill and moved on as he pleased. The people liked to feed him when they could only stroke him in return. And he also enjoyed the petting very much.

It was quite different with dogs, which seemed to be made for the service of humans and had to pander for their food and perform all kinds of tricks. Dogs got nothing for free and had to make a lot of effort for food and some affection. This culminated in a practice, which he had often observed to his astonishment: the dozens of times repeated return of an object that the owner had deliberately thrown away again and again; usually a branch. Stunned, the cat took note of this undignified spectacle. How could one be so humiliated for a little canned food? He would never lower himself to something so obviously useless.

It seemed to him as if people kept their dogs for amusement. This concept was completely incomprehensible to him, as it was the other way around with cats: people do not choose their cats to be amused. Cats choose their humans to be served and cuddled – and to let people share in their splendor. That was the way this cat wanted it, and he was determined to choose his humans in this village.

But he had very specific ideas: He did not want too many children, who would continuously try to pull his tail. But he also did not want too many old people, who would try to stroke him all the time. He was repelled by noise as well as by deathly silence. There should not be too much or too little attention. Typical for cats, he was demanding and choosy. He unsuccessfully looked through many windows and saw many unsuitable people.

Finally, he found a promising house at the end of the last road. A man was standing in front of the terrace and chopping wood. A woman could be seen through the kitchen window, busy with god knows what. Both looked friendly and smiled at each other through the window. They were probably the parents of two almost grown-up children who were passing the time in the living room. The daughter was lying on the sofa while the son was sitting cross-legged in front of the TV. It was a completely ordinary scene, which the cat liked very much. He decided to take a closer look at the family and searched for a sheltered place with a good view of the house and garden. From there he could watch the calm activity the whole afternoon. When the lights came on in the evening, he could see what was going on in the house even better. The cat liked what he saw. The special thing about this family was how normal they seemed.

In the meantime, they had gathered around the dining table and were conversing. An intensive discussion could be observed. The cat wanted to know more and sat down directly at the glass door that led from the living room into the open air. He did not think that he could be seen in the dark. However, his eyes reflected the flickering light of the fireplace and so it did not take long until the family noticed him and interrupted their animated conversation abruptly. All four inhabitants of the house stared at him spellbound, without saying a word.

3 – A noble creature

As an orphan, he had grown up without brothers or sisters on a farm on the edge of a village. His world had encompassed a house, a stable and a tool shed. All kinds of animals lived there and were well cared for by the farming family, who spent most of their time in the fields. A donkey, two cows, three pigs, four sheep and a countless amount of poultry populated this manageable piece of earth. Rodents of every color, found a comfortable shelter here as well. However, the undisputed boss was the farm dog.

The donkey was kindly yet abused as a beast of burden. The cows were indeed sensitive and strong, but were milked continuously. The pigs were clever, but lived in their own slop. The sheep were open-minded and sociable, but were shorn in steady regularity, robbing them of their fur. The chickens were curious and friendly, but got their eggs stolen every day anew. And many were intended for the plate at the next best opportunity. Although they were all peace loving, they were all exploited – perhaps for that very reason.

The dog, however, was on top. He was petted, would never end up in the cooking pot and thanked this with legendary loyalty. The other animals had equal measures of hate and fear for this barker. It was the one who called them to order, barking, growling and biting, whenever the situation required it. The dog was the farmer's extended arm and thus a forerunner of this exploitative system.

The little tomcat was on his own in this cutthroat world. He got nothing from the farmer. No attention and no food. The farmer did not care that the little cat, like all little kittens, was sweet as sugar. He was not stroked, not picked up and carried around on his arms. Not cuddled and kissed on the head. He was pushed around and pushed aside in the stable with heavy rubber boots until he sat behind the pigs in the dung heap. He was lucky not to have been drowned in the rain barrel or thrown against the wall like other cat babies. It was his privilege to be allowed to live. He had to take care of everything else himself and in the beginning he only lived on what he happened to find. Besides stable mice, this was also what was left in the troughs of other farm animals.

He fended for himself, ate whatever he could get in front of his snout and slept here and there. He made friends with some of the animals, if he expected something from them, others he preferred to avoid. He especially avoided the dog and never went to its bowl. The dog was not only dangerous. On top of that, it was hardly an honorable creature: A tyrant towards the other animals of the farm, but at the same time pure subservience: to do everything the master demanded, to walk by foot, to come when called, to sleep in a miserable hut next to the stable and to guard the farm for nights, only to give his paw in the morning, wagging his tail. The cat would never eat this pathetic puppet's leftovers!

Fortunately for him, this was not necessary, because he learned quickly. He very patiently practiced hunting and became more skillful with every mouse he caught. Soon the tomcat was no longer dependent on the remains of other animals and caught his prey himself.

His radius of movement increased. Soon he was fast enough to catch small hares in the adjacent field and strong enough to hunt martens. Rodents could not penetrate the furry armor and were exposed to his attacks. He knew to camouflage himself and to sneak up. One could hardly see him coming from far away, or even hear him. Completely in contrast to the arrogant mutt, whose claws produced so loud scratching noises on the flagstones that only someone deaf could have overheard. And then there is the permanent barking! This noisy dog, which ran around incessantly, was a thorn in the cat's side.

Over time, the cat became faster, stronger and more agile, until finally he was independent and truly self-sufficient. He did not need anybody and derived great pride from this. He became a loner and liked to sit up in the hayloft, from where he could look down on the other animals and watch the colorful hustle and bustle in the stable. He thought he was smarter than the other animals on the farm, and since his strength grew quickly, he wanted to be more than just an observer. If it went on like this, he could send the farm dog to hell one day. He was sure of that. "I'll show that pompous vermin," he thought to himself. The other animals sensed the growing resentment against the dog and hoped for liberation. But the cat did not want to free the other animals of the farm. He had no pity for them, because for him they were just simple-minded usefulness. No, he rather wanted to have the say himself!

One day, he felt strong enough to take over the helm and dared to challenge the dog. In the basement of the house, he climbed on a chair between two kegs of beer and waited for his adversary. When the dog was within reach, he gave a loud scream and jumped on him with open claws. The dog flinched and instinctively took flight. The tomcat rushed after it and chased the king of the yard once across its turf. But the dog got up his strength after he had overcome the initial fright and it was clear that the attacker was only the then still young tomcat. The cocky one was no danger. The dog turned around and gave the tomcat some paw blows that he would not forget so quickly. Thrown to the ground, bleeding scratches, hit hard at the end of the right hind leg. In the middle of the yard, right in front of the tool shed with its three arches, the revolt ended before it really began.

So for the time being, there was no getting past the dog. The tomcat had developed magnificently, but in a serious fight he would not have had much to oppose the dog's teeth and claws. The robust animal had only taught him a lesson and would tear him to pieces if necessary. He would have to subordinate himself if he wanted to stay. So he decided to leave. Out into the wilderness, into the unknown, far away from home.

In the beginning, the injury that the dog had inflicted on his hind leg still hindered him. He dragged his right leg a little bit and left a small trace in the ground with every step. However, this light limp took neither strength nor tension from the tomcat. And since it did not kill him, it had to make him stronger. He was certainly not the first whose sense of self-interest was sharpened by physical adversity.

His journey had begun. His thoughts were like his body and wandered restlessly. He was free. And he grew.

4 – The welcoming family

Nobody knew exactly when the family had come to the area, but it must have been a long time ago. Much was known about the previous generations from the elder's many tales. The family memory went back as far as the stagecoach era. Beyond that, however, the memory faded because there were hardly any records or memorabilia from what came before.

The great-great-grandfather had left behind the oldest documents still preserved. Photographs that seemed ancient and were at the same time astonishingly contemporary. They showed a man who was in the prime of his life over a century ago, but who was not unlike today's everyman. Casting a proud pose, he presented himself with his most important tool, a plow. He was the first family member whose face was thus captured for posterity. And he was the last one who still worked in the fields and, in the sweat of his brow, wrung from nature the fruits with which he earned his meager living. As a farmer, he had to be many things: Field worker and meteorologist, farrier and mechanic, warehouse clerk and market crier. He was probably, like so many of his guild, also a distiller by the way. He was always bound to the calendar, which structured the year from sowing to harvest. He owed his livelihood to the triad of earth, rain and sun.

The great-grandfather who followed him was then the first to break through this constant rhythm of the seasons. The new measure of time was the steam engine. Day in, day out, it moved huge millstones. Hissing and pounding alternated regularly in rapid succession. With deafening noise, wind and water were displaced as the source of power for the many small mills that had previously existed everywhere. Since the introduction of the new engines, there were only a few mills, but they were all the larger. These allowed huge quantities of grain to be reliably processed into flour. The monotonous daily work of a miller was sweaty and dangerous. Clothing could get caught in a belt at any time, and drag the wearer relentlessly into the interior of the roaring machine. Quite a few paid for a mishap with their lives. In such a case, those who were only mutilated were fortunate. That the steam engine was later replaced by an electric one hardly reduced the dangers. However, the advantages of the new working world were considerable: specialization allowed higher wages and more goods to be produced. So the great-grandfather was able to build up a modest wealth. He was the first in the family to have regular working hours as well as something like leisure activities.

The grandfather seized his chance in his younger years when a large automobile factory opened nearby. He got an apprentice-ship and rose quickly. Machines punched and bent sheet metal, which was then welded or riveted together by workers. People were subordinates of the assembly line, which, like a metro-nome, controlled every movement. In countless work steps, seemingly just as countless cars were created. They existed in the most diverse forms, but they were indistinguishable in their quality. Standardization and automation made enormous prog-ress possible. The profits were passed to the people with the sup-port of the unions. The grandfather was the first in the family to have his own car, health insurance and all sorts of electrical gad-gets. Even the annual summer vacation was now normal. People were very well provided for.

The father grew up in this prosperity, but could hardly imag-ine monotonous work in the factory. He was the first to graduate from college and worked as an accountant for a consumer elec-tronics manufacturer. He earned good money for many years and the family was doing well. They had two cars and three tele-visions. Or was it three cars and two televisions? He could no longer say exactly, because the amount of consumer goods had become quite confusing.

A few years ago, however, this changed abruptly. When the competition on the world markets intensified, the company underwent a so-called transformation. The factory closed and reopened in a country where workers were industrious and undemanding. Moreover, even there, the bookkeeping was probably now done by computer. The well-paid jobs were irretrievably lost. The father was the unnecessary remnant of a vanished industry. He felt like a fax machine in a travel agency. Outdated and incompatible. Old stock. And since there were few alternatives in his home town, the father did not have many options left. So he hired on, for better or worse, at a fast food restaurant on the thoroughfare. As shift supervisor, he was able to pay the most important bills, but significant moves up were no longer possible. Finding a lucrative job at his age was nothing less than illusory, as the entire region had been in a downturn for years.

Like his, many other jobs migrated to developing countries full of young people hungry for success. The domestic economy came under pressure and with it the stock markets. So the family had even lost a large part of their savings in a slide in stock prices, which experts euphemistically called a correction. Hopelessness had spread.

To top it all off, heating oil was expensive, because the demand was great in this particularly cold winter. Fortunately, they had enough trees on their plot to produce a lifetime's worth of firewood. Father and son took turns chopping for days at a time. Today it was the father's turn to split the logs, which were only roughly cut with a chain saw, into handy logs. He used an axe to cut the pieces in half until they finally reached a size that would fit into the small fireplace in the living room. With each stroke of the axe, he exhaled firmly, which immediately produced a small white cloud. Sweat steamed up from his sweater. He was busy for a good hour, until enough wood was prepared for the evening and the night. Now only the fire had to be lit and a cozy evening with wife and children could begin. Even though the latter probably still needed convincing.

"Daddy, close the door!"

"Yeah, sure, just one more basket. Then it will last until tomorrow morning. Give me a hand!"

The son got up reluctantly. It was easier for the two of them to carry the heavy basket into the house together. The stack of wood next to the stove was quickly raised by the logs that had just been brought in. Now the wood was neatly draped in the oven. First, thin sticks were placed in the middle, only slightly larger than a long match. Then the father placed wider and wider pieces on top of them until the thick logs were placed on the outside like the poles of a tepee. If the small, inner pieces were now lit, the flames would gradually spread to the larger logs and reliably ignite a cozy fire. It succeeded at the first try. Warmth filled the living room, accompanied by a soothing flicker. Outside, darkness set in early and a delicious smell from the kitchen announced the upcoming dinner.

"What's for dinner?" cried the daughter from the sofa towards the kitchen, while the men celebrated archaically, happy to have started a fire.

"Noodle soup with peas," the mother replied.

"Again?"

"Not so sassy, young lady! Give me a hand and start making the salad." The daughter had little desire to follow the request because almost every evening it was her job to mix the dressing with the salad immediately before the meal so it would not collapse.

The daughter announced her intention to soon begin the process of putting herself into motion with a practiced and drawn-out "in-a-second!"

The father turned away from the fire and firmly said, "Help your mother and don't look so annoyed!"

The daughter slowly rose from her half-prone, half-sitting position, where she could remain motionless for hours, looking at the tiny screen in her hands. When she was engrossed in something, she reluctantly put the device out of her hand to make herself useful. Nobody really knew who she was chatting with, what she was playing or which app was trendy at the moment. One could only tell by the look on her face that she was winning or losing a game, that she was upset during a chat duel, or that she was bored again, drifting through the ocean of trivialities like a boat without a rudder. Surfing, which suggests a certain excitement, would surely look differently. Her facial expression changed like in a flipbook in slow motion. A lazy afternoon on her phone seemed to be an effective remedy for the burden of reality.

In contrast to his sister, the son was enthusiastic about sports. In the summer, outdoor practice predominated, where he measured his physical strength against his friends' every day in the fight for the ball. Now in winter, however, theory prevailed and he sharpened his reactions while playing on the console. After days at the controller, he won game after game. On this evening, the championship was once again within reach. First the gathering of firewood and shortly afterwards the dinner forced him to postpone his ceremony for the time being.

"Dinner is ready! Are you coming?" the mother shouted to her men. Father and son said yes and sat down at their usual places at the dining table.

Mother and daughter had prepared the plates in the kitchen and carried two out each. A drawn-out "Enjoy your meal!" was said by both almost simultaneously as they put the plates down. An equally extended "Thank you" was answered by the men in unison. As if to assure herself of her position as chef, the mother added another "Bon appetit!"

Everyone began to eat in silence. When after a few bites no one spoke up, the mother began to have doubts. "Do you like it?"

"Yes, but it was better the last time," slipped out of the father, who had to know that he was on thin ice.

The mother turned red. A vertical vein emerged on her forehead. "Don't you like it?"

"Yes, it is really good! I'm just teasing you a little."

"Very funny."

"Don't be that way," said the father. "It tastes really good."

"Okay," said the mother and continued to eat.

The situation had been stabilized and a family conversation began, as it probably happened a million times in the country right then.

From "How was school?" and "How is it supposed to be? Boring," to "But my friends all have tattoos," up to "Sit up straight!" everything was there. The evergreen "The weather these days!" had to make an appearance, too. "That's right, I have never seen so much snow ..."

"Oh yes! It's just plain cold. I'm really looking forward to the summer vacation," said the daughter beaming with joy.

"You know exactly what it looks like right now," replied the father. "But I'm sure we can manage a nice week at the lake."

"Gee, Dad! Can't we fly somewhere sunny again?" asked the daughter.

"You can get a tan at the lake just as well!"

A lively discussion developed about where they should go for their next summer vacation, which would perhaps be the last one together before the children moved out. Everybody wanted something different, but especially the mother felt it was important to go together once more.

"Maybe you will soon be on your own! Wouldn't you like to go away with us again?" As there was no answer, she grabbed her daughter's arm and said "Hello? Aren't you listening to me?"

The daughter looked past her mother, spellbound, and pointed to the glass door leading into the garden. "Look there!"

Their gazes wandered in the direction indicated by her finger. No sound escaped the open mouths. There stood the cute orange tomcat with thickly puffed fur, defying the cold. Motionless, and without blinking, he looked at the family. No ill intentions could be detected in his appearance and the attentive, friendly look of his big round eyes seemed to captivate the family.

"Oh, he's so cute," the son finally said.

A confused mixture of voices erupted and nobody understood anyone.

"Just listen," the daughter drowned out everyone else. "Don't we want to let him in? It's really cold outside!"

"Sure!" cried the son, jumped up and ran to the door. When he opened it, the cat paused for a moment to add a little more drama to his performance. Then he ran over and wiggled wildly around the legs of each family member. He stretched out his chin in greeting and placed it about in the middle of the shin. He then slid the side of his head along the lower leg until his neck reached the calf. Everyone stroked him and was thrilled. He was pawed from head to tail, taken up, cuddled and passed on.

"He is totally soft!" said the son.

"Really cute," added the daughter. "Do we want to keep this one?"

"We can't throw him out in the cold, can we?" said the father and looked at his wife questioningly.

"I don't know. In the end I'll have to get rid of the hair …," she replied. "Don't you think we should let him out again?"

There was no need to answer. Three people and a cat looked at her with glowing eyes. She was convinced. "Okay, we'll leave him inside for now and see what happens. What do we have to lose?"

"That's right," the cat thought. "What do you have to lose?"

5 – Glad again

The rest of the evening was all about the fluffy guest. Everyone wanted to stroke the cat. He explored all corners of the house, hopped on the table, from there to the shelf and back again. The fact that his right hind leg was still limping a bit only increased his ambition. He was in a good mood and even managed to jump from the armrest of the sofa onto the cupboard.

"Wow! Did you see that?" cried the son at the sight of the huge leap. Everyone had seen it, but no one answered. Everyone was too amazed at the power-stained skill of the four-legged friend. Of course, the leap back to the floor was flawless, too.

The tomcat enthused his hosts and nobody could wait their turn to pick him up. When the time finally came, tomcat and human being looked each other in the eyes, nose to nose. His penetrating gaze and the deep purring were captivating.

The daughter took him in her arms and swayed him motherly back and forth. "It's completely crazy. When he looks at me like that, I feel a tingling in my stomach. Totally intense!"

"Give me that little guy," said the father, and grabbed the cat. But he did not like to be touched by all people at the same time.

Purring became hissing. "HHHHISSSS!!!!!"

"Wow! He has another side to him! Well, I better wait a little longer." The father laughed, but preferred to keep his hands to himself, so as not to risk getting scratched.

Being touched from the side without being asked did not go down well with the tomcat. Especially when he was already being held by someone. He preferred to approach people on his own and win each heart individually. And so it went around several times. He hopped on the shoulders of one of them and nestled himself to their head. He pressed his forehead against the next one's hand while jumping up slightly with his front paws. He stroked one of them over the cheek without extending his claws, gently biting the other one's toe. Everybody got what they wanted – several times over with pleasure.

The whole time he puffed up his fur and was wonderfully soft. "It's soooo cuddly," said the father enthusiastically. "I've never felt anything like it. Like a cotton ball!"

"Ha-ha. You're the cotton ball here, Daddy," said the daughter laughing and pressed the father lightly in his stomach.

"Yeah, sure! You just make fun of me." He grinned broadly at his daughter. The mood was exuberant and the family laughed a lot. The presence of the cat seemed to do the people good. He did not like the fact that they all repeatedly stuck their noses into his fur to smell him, but he took it easy – he wanted to make the best possible impression and be accepted by the family. And if people liked his smell, it played into his furry paws.

However, it was not just the family that was studying him. He was also studying the family. And his first impression was very promising. He did not seem to be mistaken and assumed to have hit the bull's eye here. Within these four walls, there was a great longing for harmony and confidence. Perhaps he would be able to bring these people together. This way, he would win them over and be showered with rich gifts. With a little luck, he would always have a full plate from now on.

As the evening turned into night, it was time to go to bed. Everybody would have liked to have the little furry beast with them, even if he would have managed to take half the width of the mattress. He would have been free to choose whose bed he would occupy, and who would have to dislocate in an effort to get a corner of the blanket. But on the first night he did not want to signal that he had a favorite person. He preferred to let the family fidget a bit and lie down on the living room cupboard for the night. From there the view was especially good and he felt sublime and protected.

The following day began as the last one had ended. It was weekend and the family had all time in the world to get to know the cat. Everyone gathered around the cute little guy and the hours were entertaining. The tomcat did some mischief and conquered the hearts.

His positive attitude was transferred to the residents. Whether the tomcat clung to the father's legs as he swept the snow away in front of the house, or whether he *helped* the mother with the cooking and carefully snagged a small piece of meat from the pot with his sharp claws to lick it off his paw with relish before her eyes. Extensive cuddling peppered with little pranks were his recipe for success. And even the youngsters stopped using their cell phones and computer games at times when the cat was around. If he did not immediately get the attention he deserved, he would either sit down on the keyboard or directly in front of the monitor to force an occupation with him. But nobody could be angry with him, because everybody loved those little disturbances. And everyone would have wanted the weekend to last a bit longer. But now it was Sunday evening, and after the common meal the family wanted to discuss how to proceed with the little guest.

The father had already made himself comfortable in the living room and was waiting impatiently for the rest of the family. "Everyone come over for the family powwow," resounded through the house. The mother rolled her eyes, but sat down right next to her husband and laid her head lovingly on his shoulder. Unusually fast for teenagers, they both followed the call and sat down around the crackling hearth.

"We want to keep him!" cried the daughter before anyone else could say anything. "That's right – we're both in favor," the son quickly added, to make it clear that the two agreed.

"It was really funny, wasn't it? I'd also say we'll leave him here for now." The father seemed to have noticed his wife's skeptical look. "What do you think?"

"I don't know, he's really cute. But in the end, I'll be the one to clean up the mess. Everything will be on me again. Just like

Jonny!" The mother pointed to a small cage in the corner of the living room. A slightly neglected, fat hamster lived there. Obviously, he hardly received anyone's attention anymore. "I am the only one here who at least provides him with food and water. You wanted to have him, and now I have to take care of him," said the mother in an unmistakably reproachful tone toward her children.

The son begged for understanding: "But this is different! Jonny is just hanging around. You can't do anything with him. And when you pick him up, he bites."

"That's right. Jonny is just a hamster. But the cat is really cool!" the daughter added.

"And you forgot the dog already, didn't you?" asked the mother. "Lex just died a few weeks ago, and now you suddenly want a cat?"

"We haven't forgotten Lex at all!" said the daughter indignantly.

"Exactly. Besides, a tomcat is something completely different from a dog," the son added.

"And you certainly don't want another dog? Maybe sometime in the summer?" asked the mother. "A dog and a cat do not get along very well. You can't have both!"

"No," said the daughter. "We don't want a new dog. Lex was our dog and we don't want to replace her with another one."

"That's right, we can try the cat, can't we? He is here now and it's totally fun with him. Please," said the son, and looked at his parents alternately with puppy dog eyes.

The father took the children's side. "You saw how much good he's done us. We laughed together the whole weekend. The whole time we were busy with him and forgot all our worries. I think he can make our family glad again!"

"Perhaps you are right. Let's give it a try then. But hopefully there won't be any quarrels over who cleans up after him! Maybe we'll have to educate him a bit if he's too much of a pain in the ass!"

"It won't be so bad, sweetheart!"

"Let's hope so! Promise you'll help me if he's a handful?"

"Yes, yes, yes," the three of them sang in unison.

"Okay, I'll remind you then," the mother closed the discussion.

The family powwow was over and the furry guest became a furry family member. He found it funny that the family now thought they had chosen him, since he had chosen the family at least as much. He had also used the weekend to assess the value of the family for his progress. Would he benefit from staying in the family, or should he rather keep looking? Going back out into the wild, cold and self-sufficiency, or would he rather stay here and wait for spring?

He decided for the latter, because he liked the all-round service he was offered. If it was no longer practical to stay, he could leave at any time. But for now he enjoyed the amenities: The mother provided him with the best food he had ever had. With the greatest hustle and bustle, the son invented games and adventures for him. The daughter had a remarkable stamina for stroking and combing his fur. And the father had placed a wonderful wooden log in the living room for him to have a place to stretch and scratch. They had all let him out countless times when he needed fresh air, only to let him back in again shortly afterwards when he was cold. With all this begging, one would soon think that he was the pet that depended on the family and completely ignored that they were in fact his vehicle into the fully comprehensive life – an extremely convenient source of constant care and recognition. He was not alone with this view of people. All cats try to instrumentalize humans for their own purposes with varying degrees of luck. But only one was as successful as the orange cat wanted to be: His old pal and role model Monty.

He had met Monty on a late autumn evening a couple of months before, when the weather was dry and the colorful foliage on the slope of a terraced vineyard was shining. At the foot of these hills were several picturesque lakes, with a village in between. He was dreamily strolling halfway up the hill when suddenly an impressively large tomcat, whose stature resembled more that of a small bear, jumped out from between the vines and blocked the path.

"Where are you going, young fellow?" Monty asked in a language that only animals understand.

"Nowhere," he replied. "I just roam the woods and fields and don't really know where to go yet."

Monty looked skeptically under his eyebrows. "You don't know where you are going?"

"I roam and enjoy the beauty of autumn."

Monty nodded his broad head slowly.

"To march alone through the autumn forest," the orange one said, "is the greatest thing a cat can experience!"

Monty still nodded. "You're right, my boy. But the first leaves are already changing from yellow to brown. Soon it will be winter. And that's not a good time to march through the forest alone."

"I don't think about that today," he replied. "It's the most beautiful time of the year and I enjoy the casualness of freedom!"

Monty was still nodding. "You are right, my boy. But do you have a family where you can spend the winter?"

"I did, but I prefer the bittersweet scent of liberty. Nothing to tie you down. You can't live with more immediacy," he said with firm conviction, "I'll see what winter brings."

Monty stopped nodding and looked serious. "You'll really appreciate a warm place. Was it that bad with your family?"

"I was under the lash of a dog and his human trainers. A pitiful alliance. Until the end, I tried to fathom what was more reprehensible: the submissiveness of the quadruped or the presumptuousness of the biped."

"Oh, that's easy!" Monty laughed aloud. "The dog is merely a whinnying, self-deprecating wretch, unworthy even of contempt. Man, however, is an impostor and a simpleton of the very first order! He commands every movement of his faithful dog, but he secretly longs for the strength of character of a true tomcat!"

"True words," he agreed.

"Wait! It gets worse! If man is finally granted the honor of having a cat in the house, he imagines it can be tamed. But he does not even notice how he himself is tamed by the cat."

"Did you manage that? Have you tamed your family?"

"Oh yes! It works wonderfully. Believe me, one day I'll get the people to fetch me a stick," Monty said calmly and took a measured break. "To answer your question, humans are even more reprehensible than dogs. Their hubris is truly shameful. But you can hibernate very well with them. Come with me, I'll show you!"

And so the tomcat with the shiny copper coat followed his almost fatherly looking new friend Monty on his way down to the valley. He was very excited to explore his world and the tension grew inside him with every step. He lost all sense of the environment, which was particularly lovely and varied in this region. The sunshine had brought the stone slabs lying around everywhere to a pleasant temperature, so that it was difficult for a tomcat not to lie down on them and let his gaze wander until the inevitable hunger would force him to take action. On this day, however, everything was different and it was impossible to think of a pause. Monty set the pace with his long strides and went quickly towards the village between the lakes.

Unlike in other areas, which the cat had roamed before, the paths here became more riddled by potholes the closer one came to the village. They finally reached the farm, which Monty proudly showed as if it was his own. It consisted of a narrow but very long plot of land with a house in the middle, which was large and time-honored, but had been needing a new coat of paint for some time. The family obviously had other priorities than maintaining the appearance of their house. Even urgently needed maintenance measures seemed to have been postponed for some time. In several places, holes in the plaster exposed the brickwork. A drainpipe that slipped out of the gutter leaned at an angle against a wall and offered a small family of sparrows ideal conditions for nest-building. The feisty little birds were certainly as indifferent to the condition of the building as were the people living in it. But they certainly enjoyed the wonderfully arranged and extraordinarily well-kept garden just as much. The hedges were meticulously maintained and the trees were overflowing with ripe stone fruit. A man could be seen standing on a ladder harvesting countless peaches and carefully placing them in a basket. These people seemingly liked to spend time outside.

But even before the cat's eyes captured the first details, two other senses revealed that the cats were getting closer to their destination. An indecipherable babble of voices trying to drown out each other, coupled with the incredibly inviting smell of a freshly prepared lunch, could be sensed from afar. As they turned the corner, their eyes fell on an extravagant seating arrangement, on whose table a fashionable lady was draping dishes and cutlery. She was arguing with a wildly gesticulating young woman who seemed to be her daughter. A young man, probably the woman's son, stood next to her, juggling a ball with his feet, and occasionally joined in the conversation. The older man climbed down from his ladder, commenting on the event while carrying the rich harvest to the house. The orange cat was amazed. How could four people make such a noise?

When the family discovered Monty, they fell silent abruptly and stared at him motionless. He winked at them slowly and kindly, whereupon they hurriedly gathered around the table, filled their plates and began to eat. Only the daughter did not take part, but rattled away with an infernal noise on a motor scooter. Her absence was probably the subject of the loud argument. Or had it simply been a typical conversation in this family? It was not necessarily clear to an outsider.

But there was no doubt that Monty was the head of the family. He was given his own seat at the front of the table, the largest piece of meat on the most beautiful plate, and was alternately cuddled by his neighbors to the right and left. Monty loved to be cuddled during the meal.

After the meal, Monty proudly showed the house where he had his own room as a private retreat. There was a velvet-covered sofa and a huge scratching post for Monty to sharpen his claws. From summer to early fall, a fresh bouquet of catnip was placed in his room every day, the smell of which stimulated and soothed him. In the garden, the plant was grown in a large bed especially for Monty, so that the supply was always ensured.

"In winter there will only be dried catnip, unfortunately, which the daughter of the house collects and sews into small pillows. I would like to have it fresh all year round. But unfortunately I have not yet succeeded in influencing the rhythm of nature in addition to the daily routine of people." Monty laughed proudly.

And the daily routine seemed to revolve around Monty to a large extent, because there was always a family member busy doing good for him. The whole day seemed to be a never-ending parade of comforts. Father and son seemed to adore Monty and took great pleasure in looking after his well-being. Monty's unexpected guest was also warmly welcomed and treated like their own. The two were extensively petted by father and son as they chatted over afternoon coffee. So they were constantly stroked with the free hand of the coffee drinker sitting closest to them. There was also a lot of sweet cream pudding, which was enjoyed as an afternoon snack. The two tomcats each got their share and preferred to eat it straight from the spoon.

The woman was not part of the relaxed cup of coffee. Maybe she distrusted Monty. At any rate, she eluded the fuss around the big cat, who commanded her respect with his huge claws and sharp teeth. And so she looked after Monty more like a reliable chambermaid than as a faithful admirer. Like the other family members, she stroked him briefly when she passed him but only reluctantly touched his head. She then tentatively stretched her arm as far as possible and scratched Monty on the area under his chin, which he tried to enlarge by placing his head in the neck. Monty liked her obvious respect for his sharp biting tools.

Otherwise, the woman left the two tomcats to themselves all afternoon while she fulfilled her domestic duties. She removed cat hair from the seat cushion and sofa, emptied Monty's toilet and also made sure that there was always a bowl of fresh milk to drink. Today there was even something very special: cold milk with a little strawberry sorbet stirred into it. "Here, Monty, here you go, your favorite drink! Maybe your new friend would like to try it too."

Monty formed a spoon with his rough tongue, suddenly dipped it into the delicious drink and then slung a small portion into his mouth. More than a little splashed on the whiskers as well as the surrounded fur and dripped from there back into the bowl, from where it was taken up again by the tongue shortly after – it was not the fastest way to drink. Monty obviously loved it, for he almost forgot to share the treat with his new friend. Only when the floral pattern at the bottom of the bowl already showed, did he stop his greedy slobbering.

"Oh, excuse me, pal! Please, try it once. It is a fountain of youth!" Monty grinned at him, "It tastes and has always been good for vigor."

He did not have to be asked twice, forming his tongue into a spoon as well, he tasted the reddish potion in the same lavishly sloppy manner. After a few blows of the tongue, he turned away in horror: "Yuck!" This must have been a very good fountain of youth, if he were to drink just one more sip of it.

"Is it not satisfying your exquisite taste?" asked Monty.

"No," he assured him, "it is fantastic!"

Then Monty made a face. "Hmm, the only thing I can offer you otherwise is water with a splash of orange."

"Sounds good! How do we get it?"

Monty's grin came back. "Now you can learn something."

Then the big black cat turned his head towards the woman and hissed briefly. With his eyes, he indicated a basket of fruit that was resting on the table. The woman seemed to understand. She cut an orange in half and pressed its juice into a feeding bowl. Diluted with some water, she put the drink down with her head bowed in front of the two tomcats.

"You see, it's as simple as that," said Monty. "Why do you look so perplexed? Just start drinking!"

Slowly he began to slobber. He did not notice at that moment whether the taste was better or worse. He was still too amazed by how Monty got his way. It was probably the well-tempered climate of adoration, spiced with a pinch of fear, which made people recognize and fulfill Monty's wishes. If something did not happen on its own, a stern look or a brief hiss was enough. If something went against his grain, Monty, who was almost as big as a puma, impressively demonstrated his aversion with the smallest gesture. It only took a short twitch of his tail to show the humans their place. A short showing of teeth was also not mistaken for a smile. A slightly implied paw stroke was a particularly effective means to make people come to their senses – Monty only had to lift one paw briefly. And since nobody wanted to risk a bite or scratch, everyone acted accordingly.

However, such stages of escalation hardly seemed necessary. Most of it was automatic. For example, the daughter arrived later that afternoon on the scooter with a large shopping basket full of groceries on its carrier. Her first stop was not at the refrigerator, as one would have expected, but to the two cats. She placed half a sausage in front of each of them and brushed briefly over their foreheads. "Here, enjoy your meal," she said before she disappeared into the house to stow the rest of the food away. And although they were still full from the cream pudding, they complied with the request and enjoyed the little meat snack. "To get a tasty sausage just like that," he thought to himself and said, "Maybe it's not so bad with the right family."

Monty looked him calmly in the eyes. "Without a doubt, this family is great, my boy! But they have their flaws." His face darkened as he continued: "Not only are they loud. Their character defects are superficiality, recklessness and the belief that everything will work out fine. They are a herd of sheep that would fall apart without me. And because they know that, they love me." The contempt in his voice was unmistakable.

"With all due respect. I didn't get the impression that everyone loved you. The woman was extremely suspicious and reserved. I think she was even afraid of you. With your imperious ways, I'm sure you'll make her your enemy one day."

"So many enemies, so much honor," Monty replied briskly. "Besides, this family needs me to get ahead. Nothing happens here without me. Whenever these people try to decide something together, it ends in deception, fraud or farce! The truth is that these people are tired of freedom!"

"And then you decide?"

"Exactly. Only then will it move forward."

"But do you really think one cat alone can lead a whole family?"

Insatiable ambition flashed in Monty's eyes. "Of course I do! It even *only* works when the cat is on his own! A tomcat always becomes particularly strong when he has no one to rely on. It is good to trust others, but not to do so is even better!" Monty took a heavy pause, gathered himself and looked deeply into the eyes of his young guest. "Do you think we tomcats have daggers in our mouths for no reason, spikes on our paws and contempt in our hearts?"

"Certainly not, but other animals also have ..."

Monty interrupted him with a very firm voice. "Of course they do! But a family needs a leader! Someone who gives it a concept, a function, a goal. A dog can't do that."

"Only a big, strong cat can," he said.

"Now you got it, my boy," Monty concluded the conversation. No further words were needed. The two winked at each other meaningfully, as only cats can, calmly and confident of their own superiority. So they lay quietly behind the house for some time, looking into the garden and letting themselves be scratched, while occasionally biting into the long blades of grass growing out of the pavement in front of them, slowly turning their heads back and forth around all axes. Suddenly Monty said, "I'll tell you my winning formula."

His excitement left silence as the only answer.

"I know their language!"

With disbelief, silence remained the answer.

"You can believe it. I have learned to speak the language of the people. It is a rather simple form of expression, but I know it," Monty assured.

He felt mocked. "That is completely impossible! You're joking!"

"I'll show you." Monty got up and stood up in front of the two men who were still sitting in their garden chairs. They interrupted their conversation and looked at Monty expectantly. They seemed to suspect something. And then it happened:

"Crrraaate," Monty hissed.

The men laughed loudly and hopped excitedly up and down. "He's speaking again! Mamma, come here. Monty is speaking," the son yelled in the direction of the house. "Come on, say it again, Monty!"

"Crrraaate!" he hissed more clearly.

"He wants his box! Mamma, bring the box out! Hurry up!"

"Crrraaate," Monty repeated once more, thereby emphasizing his demand.

By then, the mother came running out of the house nervously with a huge, empty cardboard box. Due to the hurry with which she carried it, the ends, yielding to the wind pressure, opened - right into her face. She stopped briefly, opened the box wide and then carefully placed it under the garden table. Despite its size, it was actually too small for the huge cat. But Monty loved lying down in his box, no matter how over-sized he was. He protruded over the edge on all sides and bent the cardboard so much that it began to tear. The good feeling of lying in a box was only increased by the fact that it was also under a table. A cave-like feeling. It could hardly be more beautiful. In the box, under the table and full to the brim – a cat's ultimate good fortune.

The men were also happy to fulfill their tomcat's wish. That he talked to them, no matter how short the formulas, delighted them. They did not notice that the woman could not share their enthusiasm. She stood stunned by the scene.

"What if at some point he wants more than a box, or something to eat? What do we do then?" she finally shouted to her men.

"Oh honey, calm down! This is a lot of fun," her husband replied.

"That's a huge tomcat and not a lot of fun! He probably weighs half a ton and can tear us apart if he wants to!"

"But he won't!"

Then the woman began to shout in a whisper: "Not yet! But what do you think is going on in the mind of a cat who can talk? Probably more than in yours!" She waved them off, ran back into the house with a red head and slammed the door.

This spectacle left the orange tomcat speechless. It repeated several times in similar form before he finally wandered back out into the wild a couple of days later. He decided, just like Monty, to learn the language of the people. Only he wanted to surpass him! Monty had become his great example and later he often thought of this impressive encounter. One day he would also have a family who would adore and fear him. But he wanted his family to adore and fear him even more.

7 – The thaw

Time flew by since the family powwow had decided some weeks ago to keep him for the time being. His days were as pleasantly composed as elevator music and consisted essentially of an endless loop of eating, cuddling and sleeping. A full stomach and extensive sleep made him so lethargic that he could not resist any attempt to stroke him. This routine was interrupted only by an occasional stretching, in which he pushed the front legs forward and his bottom up in the air with straight legs. The exercise was confusingly similar to a dislocation, which he had often seen with female humans in tight pants, and which these to his amazement called a *downward dog*. One could have also called it *downward cat*. Not to do so was typical for humans and bordered in his eyes on lèse-majesté, or treason, or heresy!

But getting upset about it would only spoil the relaxed mood and could hence wait for now. He took a deep breath and decided to educate the people on another day, because he was still happy about his pleasant existence and did not miss any effort or thrill. He would be able to endure this carefree sluggishness for quite a while, especially since his family did everything to please him. Should it become necessary, he would do it like Monty and fire them up. For now, however, he was concerned with doing nothing, because spring with all its strenuous activities would come soon enough.

Outside, a cautious thaw had set in. Warm days and cold nights started a cycle of defrosting and re-freezing. The wet surface of the snow reflected the sun's rays glittering like a lake. It seemed as if the water was still undecided about its own aggregate state.

It was the cold and wet weather that is generally rejected by cats, so he stayed in the house to watch the snow melt outside the windows. Even the grass had already appeared here and there and it was foreseeable that soon spring would drive out the lethargy of winter.

But the weather was still unstable, light and shadows, warmth and cold traded places, as quickly as the clouds flew by. A staging beautiful to watch, if you look at it from the cozy atmosphere of a heated living room. Nevertheless, the variability of the elements seemed to be transferred to the mood in the house.

The family's euphoric affection for the young, orange cat was occasionally mixed with sadness, as the former pet had only recently died. Lex the dog was still everywhere on photos on the walls. She had fallen ill just when the economic situation of the family had deteriorated. And so the expensive treatment was delayed until a cure had finally become impossible. Even desperate attempts to save her were in vain. Her decay of body and soul had progressed too far.

"You are so soft and even more cuddly than our Lex," he heard the daughter whispering, while she slowly stroked him from his head all the way down his back.

Once, when he was courting a delicious portion of cat food, the father said to his wife: "He's got those puppy-dog eyes. Just like good old Lex."

"That's right, he's cute and cuddly, but then again he hasn't scratched you yet," she warned, "Besides, I bet he's faster than Lex would have been! A cat is always faster than a dog – be careful!"

The son defended the cat. "But he has never scratched anyone! And he's not gonna!" With a sad look, he watched the cat eating. "I would not have thought that we would have a new pet so soon after Lex. Especially not a cat. But you're a great guy, aintcha?"

"Right." The father tapped his son gently on the shoulder.

Naturally, the fact that his new family kept comparing him to a dead dog displeased him. Because his superiority over dogs was so clear to him, it could only be described by strong images from epic parables. He saw himself as a David, a smaller, seemingly weaker, outsider, triumphing over the preordained winner Goliath. He was all about strength, strength of character! "These furless bipeds are so terribly one-dimensional! Useful idiots! I am certainly no faithful, dumb, do-nothing dog, no narrow-minded mutt! They will get to know me …," he thought, while he let the daughter scratch his full belly.

"You eat too much," she suddenly whispered lovingly into his ear. "You've really grown! I had hoped you would always remain so sweet and small. Maybe we should give you a little less to eat, otherwise you won't stop growing at all!" To emphasize her words, the daughter grabbed his fur with both hands and shook the cat slightly, so that his head was shaking to and fro.

He winked at her in a good-natured way and was glad that what he himself had already noticed was now also noticed by others: He had grown.

House Cat

He was no longer a little kitten. Not a rambunctious adolescent who sometimes pushes a vase off a shelf with his tail, and can hope for forgiveness because he's still so cute. He'd shot up, had grown large, resembled full-grown males in height, width and weight. Only a few weeks of rich food, care and some love had been enough to give him a growth spurt. Soon he would surpass all other cats around. For he sensed he was still growing.

8 – Lenny

One fine day, a big black tomcat was standing in the garden. His fur shiny, legs long and straight. From the inside, his calls could not to be heard through the closed windows, but they could be seen as his mouth opened in slow rhythm and released the red tongue. With each scream, his canines were exposed for a brief moment, the eyes narrowed and the whiskers bent upwards. There was no doubt that the insistent look was a demand to enter the house.

The relaxed part of the day was over for the orange master and he wondered who the stranger was. The daughter had also discovered the intruder in the garden. "Mom, there's a black cat in the garden! I think he wants to come in!"

The mother went to the window and looked out. "Oh, right! There's often been other cats in the garden since the dog died."

Suddenly, the black cat ran toward them.

"Whoa," said the daughter, leaving her mouth and eyes wide open. She forgot to scratch the orange cat on her lap, which he found kind of *whoa* as well. But he considered the fact that another cat would try to enter his family even more *whoa*. He was wide-awake and determined to prevent this.

The daughter grabbed him by the armpits and sat him down next to her on the sofa before she got up and went to the garden door. "Well, let's have a look at this little guy!"

"Oh no, not another one! We already have one!" But the mother couldn't stop her. Even before the door was open, the black tomcat stood in front of it with his tail erected and looked the daughter through the glass directly into her eyes. He jumped through the slit created as she slowly opened the door. And there he was, the rival. He looked at the furry master across the living room as amazed as the other way round.

Nothing held the orange one to the sofa anymore. He jumped

down to the floor and ran towards the black cat until he stood right in front of him. Only an inch separated their noses and both began to sniff, wagging their heads. Suspicious, they slowly turned around each other to sniff the other's smell even better – at the rear end. The tension was palpable as the two looked at each other in slow motion, trying to anticipate the next step, weighing up their own options.

Two males were facing each other, very similar in height and posture: wiry and alert. Only their fur was completely different. The black tomcat obviously pursued the classic deterrence strategy and tried to appear especially big by puffing up his fur and arching his back up. This was the oldest trick in the book. The orange one couldn't be deceived and acted completely differently on his part. He tightened his orange coat and took a powerful, crouching posture that emphasized his muscles. This tactic seemed to be unfamiliar to the newcomer and confused him, because he could think of nothing better than to emphasize his hump even more. The incumbent eased up a little. "Amateurs go by the book! What good fortune," he thought to himself.

The two women watched the scene silently and without suspecting the consequences. "They're so cute," said the daughter. "Look how they're sniffing each other," said the mother. Husband and son were waved over and now the whole family watched the first encounter of the two adversaries in the middle of their own living room. They stood eye to eye and nobody dared to blink. Both were frozen, not moving a bit. The seconds of silence passed slowly.

"How can I help you, stranger?" the orange one finally asked in the language of the animals.

"You probably couldn't," replied the challenger slowly and with a broad grin. "I'm looking for the head of the house."

"Very funny! You are standing directly in front of him! And wipe that grin off your face, or it might go away faster than you want it to!"

"Is that a threat? Or a promise?" The black tomcat remained demonstratively calm and raised his back a little further. "Maybe you should start smiling! You are so unfriendly," the stranger kept on pushing the envelope.

"And you're rude. Watch out! You're walking towards a powder keg with a burning candle."

"Actually, it seems quite cozy in here. Perhaps I'll take a closer look."

"You're not in charge here – this is my family, and this is my house!"

„Says who? It seems to me that it is not yet clear who will be in charge here in the future. I had the feeling that I had just been very kindly allowed to enter. You don't seem to be sitting very firmly in the saddle."

That truth hurt. Maybe the newcomer had been watching him and wanted to chase him away before he could really pull himself together. His nerves, like his muscles, were stretched to the limit. "You want to chase me away from my family? A well-intentioned advice, greenhorn: You better find your own family. I'm the boss here, alright?"

"Were, you mean to say. You *were* the boss here."

The orange cat's neck finally swelled. "I admire anyone who dares to punch above his weight. But someone like that can't complain about the fate that inevitably befalls every impostor!

"And what would that be?"

"You'll be kicked out."

"A threat after all. Well … if you're not mistaken! I see no weight class distinction here. I'm happy to take on a stuck-up pretender like you," the new guy said combatively.

"If you won't regret it! You know exactly: There can only be one. One family, one cat. If you mess with me, there will be war, and I will wage it more radically than you can even imagine! Do you want that?"

"You can't fight a war with silk gloves on, that's for sure."

"I have to give you credit, you are courageous to challenge me like this," he said.

"Wrong! It takes more courage to retreat than advance."

"Who the hell are you?"

"My name is Lenny."

Who the hell was this Lenny, who seemed so simple and profane, but was as militant and cunning as he himself. He was afraid that this Lenny character would cause him some more trouble. But since they were both about the same size and equally combative, the winner did not seem to be decided at all. Deterrence seemed safer to the orange master for the time being: "You should know: I have burned bridges behind me. I can't go back, but I don't want to move on either. I am forced to do the last thing and therefore determined to do the last thing. I must win."

"Well, in a fight like that, you win or you die. That goes for both of us equally," said Lenny.

"That's right. It's good that you know what you're getting into."

"I know that a fight like that isn't a dinner party and can never be so refined, so leisurely and gentle, so moderate, nice, polite, restrained and magnanimous. It is a riot, an act of violence in which one subdues the other. Don't worry – I know full well what I am getting into and I fear neither hardship nor death."

It cut him to the core. Lenny had tried the greatest possible pathos and made it clear where the journey was headed. It was going to escalate. The two tomcats turned slowly and with great caution around each other, like a dancing couple in slow motion. Only that in contrast to the dancing couple, there was no loving embrace at the end of the choreography, but possibly an uncontrolled drumfire of claws and teeth. So none of them wanted to provoke the other. Jerky movements of any kind were avoided.

"What actually makes you so sure that my family will even accept you, should you – against all expectations – defeat me? Perhaps my humans will avenge me and send you to hell."

"Nonsense!" Thrilled by his own rhetoric, Lenny replied, "They won't do that. They want to be winners themselves, so they are also attracted to winners. And that's why the loser – you – will be sent to hell. People have no pity for losers, just contempt and indifference," Lenny said.

"True, but you're forgetting one thing. My family would side with me if we'd fight. Beyond the desire to be among the winners, my people have a clear idea of what they want: A strong community under my leadership."

Lenny's grin froze and he got serious. "People have always had wrong ideas about themselves and about what should be. They have made themselves comfortable in their circumstances and want a strong leader! They cannot exist without one. At least we seem to agree on that."

"At most in this regard," the orange one made clear and paused for a while. Finally he added, "I accept the challenge! The family's gratitude shall be the winner's reward."

"Gratitude is a disease that dogs suffer from," Lenny said dismissively. "I prefer fear."

"Once again, I have to agree with you, Lenny." His similarity to his adversary was greater than he wished. They were rivals, but they were cut from the same cloth. "Once I get you out of the way, I will put the fear of God into this family ... What are you doing? Whoa ...," he shouted as his legs grew longer and longer and his paws finally left the ground.

Daughter and mother had sneaked up and grabbed the two males, lifted them up and separated them. "Otherwise there will be a disaster here," said the mother with a grin.

"The way they howled at each other. Fierce," confirmed the daughter.

"You're real brawlers!" the mother added.

The fact that he was now even compared to a pea brain rooster was the height of impudence. As if it had not been rude enough to interrupt this rich dispute so abruptly.

The two women each carried one tomcat to opposite corners
of the living room, where they were now held on the lap and
could no longer get in each other's way. But no caressing in the
world would have been able to calm their minds. He took note of
the well-meant touches, but inside he was boiling. The two tomcats looked each other suspiciously in the eyes across the room.
This conflict was anything but resolved – it was postponed for
the time being, postponed to a more suitable moment without
a referee.

9 – Jonny

Jonny watched the dispute from the corner of the living room. His cage protected the hamster from being mauled. He could only rarely leave his cage – and only under human supervision – since the arrival of the cat, and probably even when the dog still ran the show. Because of the positioning of this not self-chosen dwelling on the floor, on two sides directly adjacent to the walls, he had only a very limited view of the events through the shimmering golden bars.

As a nocturnal animal, he had an exceptionally developed sense of hearing, and since he spoke the language of the animals just like the two tomcats, he did not miss any statement, no matter how insignificant. The rodent could smell particularly well, and had a good feeling for the state of mind of dog and tomcat, too. Jonny was very close to the other pets, but would never really belong – he was too small and too weak. This certainty seemed to depress him and led him to make loud comments, often in the middle of the night, sometimes chumming up, sometimes quarrelling.

He had something to contribute to everything. Although he was an outsider, he was anything but neutral. When the orange one came into the family, Jonny screamed and jumped up and down like a chimpanzee on a tree, warning other chimpanzees when he saw a big cat coming through the woods. "OO!-OO!-AH!-OO!-OO!-AH!" His excitement was immense, but nobody seemed to pay attention to his warning cries.

A while later he seemed to have come to terms with the cat and called out to him "The dogs hate you. But you will bring them down for good," only to make his distrust known again a short time later. "I'm angry, I've had enough of you! I have seen you dancing with goblins at night! I'll come out and face you scum!" Jonny seemed crazy and had a voice that was unusually deep and rough for his small, pudgy stature.

The hamster had also noticed Lenny's arrival: "There's a new sheriff in town! OO! OO! AH! AH! A big black cat! Make sure he doesn't eat you!"

The orange tomcat smiled at the little screamer and whispered to him. "*You'd* better watch out not to get eaten. One bite and you're gone!" Shocked, Jonny took a step away from the bars. Shaking revealed his fear of the overpowering animal.

Most of the time, however, he was abandoned in his cage, talking to himself or trumpeting his fears to the world without being asked. Humans and animals did not seem to listen to him. On the contrary, they seemed rather annoyed, especially by the nightly disturbances. But there was nothing they could do about it. Jonny either ran like a wild man in his wheel until the early morning hours, or he spread his ideas loudly.

"Imagine everyone would live in peace. Imagine everyone would live in freedom," Jonny cried into the darkness, shaking the cage. "I'll topple your paradigm of absolute control!"

If he could be heard, it was usually not a subtle discussion, no stimulating presentation or fruitful dialogue. They were almost endless monologues, and since he had not only positive visions, they were tirades of fear and hate, hate and fear. He was afraid of being given poisoned water, afraid of having his claws cut off, afraid of alien people and animals, afraid of imprisonment, afraid of freedom. He hated it when the TV was on or a newspaper rustled, but most of all Jonny hated dogs and cats. The hamster did not trust anyone. And he screamed all his confused thoughts loudly through the bars of his cage into the living room. Everyone was annoyed by him.

Jonny could only rarely relax. Only when a human took him out of the cage from time to time, held him in their hand and stroked him, did he calm down, breathed slowly and became completely tame. Then he could be close to the human and felt understood. He had a good heart, his fine hearing heard overtones that others didn't, but his paranoia caused his confusion.

When Lenny appeared and argued with the orange host, Jonny watched the scene closely and listened attentively. He didn't make a sound and was highly concentrated. Because a new power struggle fired all his conspiracy theories. His imagination was fed and he painted them in the most vivid colors. He saw the great final battle for the new family order in his mind's eye and gave vent to his need to communicate.

After the two opponents were separated, Jonny shouted loudly over to Lenny: "You want war? You better believe you got one! Ha!"

"With you, you little runt?" Lenny asked incredulously.

"No, of course with the orange lump of fur! He's just as ugly as you are, and stinks of sulfur just like you. You devils! When you've torn each other to pieces, I'll do the rest! I will break out and then I'll take you on. I can fight. All my ancestors fought. Fighting is in my genes!"

Lenny was surprised and amused by the little chubby cheeks. He made a joke with Jonny: "Maybe I'll make you my deputy if you are good …"

"I see through your lies, you crazy devil!" cried Jonny. "I will never be your slave!" He was once again in a rage. "I saw a fox in the garden as I ran in my wheel this morning. He looked me in the face, winked at me as if to say 'We'll fight it'."

"Have you gone mad in captivity?" Lenny shook his head and turned away.

10 – On the other side of the fence

The combination of cold, clear air and the pleasant feeling of a coat heated up by the springtime sun boosted the spirits of life. Once again, the garden invited the tomcat to stay outside more often. Under trees and bushes lay the last remainders of snow, but where the beams of sunlight reached the ground during the day, first blossoms broke through the lawn. Long missed birds returned into these latitudes. His ornithologist heart beat faster.

Only occasionally, when rain clouds came up, did he want to get back into the house quickly to avoid wet paws. In this meteorological transition period, people were often busy opening and closing the house and garden doors to let the cats in or out. After fleeing from bad weather, he liked to check the weather on the other side of the house to make sure that it was equally bad there. The fact that the doors had to be opened more often for this purpose was an extra effort, which was gladly done. It was fun to see the cat realize that it was raining on both sides of the house.

The effort doubled, since Lenny showed similar behavior patterns. However, the two tomcats never went in or out at the same time. Instead, they avoided each other and only looked at one another from a distance. The tomcats had decided not to let their quarrel escalate for now, since both feared a crushing defeat. But it was clear as day that the hour of truth was not very far away. Both males were too ambitious and proud to give up the family without a fight. Only a good opportunity was missing, a weak moment of the opponent, or a decisive increase of their own strength.

Until the day came, both tomcats tried to win the hearts of the family for themselves - each in his own way. Lenny liked to embrace the people all together. He was not exactly an extrovert par excellence with his unadorned, plain black coat and his calm nature. But he always created a feeling of community when he jumped from lap to lap during the evening get-together and gave everyone the same portion of attention. Everyone received equally many or equally few cuddles, careful toe bites or in-ear purrs. And everyone was expected to give the same amount of effort, whether it was bringing food, petting or opening doors. The family laughed a lot together when Lenny was around, but no one felt like they were the center of attention or even his favorite person.

The orange one proceeded quite differently. He did not think much of group activities. Instead, he tried to win over each family member individually. He was adept at reading the room and gave the right impulses at the right moment. If people were cheerful, he played with them and sometimes – against his own nature – presented himself as clumsier than he was, to make them laugh. So he always started again to grab a ball of wool with a small jump, but let it slide through the claws again and again, to make the game as long as possible. Euphorically, the people threw the thread like a fishing rod through the room. If, on the other hand, children or parents were sitting helplessly in front of homework or bills, he came and gave them back their confidence in themselves. With a nudge of the nose, or by sitting down in the middle of the paper, he provided them with distraction. His good-natured gaze gave hope that one can overcome even deep valleys, if one wanted it enough. Admittedly, he could neither diminish nor solve the family's real problems in this way, but this did not stop them from rewarding his attempts at cheering them up with a bright smile and an extra portion of caresses.

In order to meet as little as possible, the two tomcats alternated impressing the family and staying outside. Only in the short moments of changing the guard did their paths cross, somewhere between inside and outside, they looked each other in the eyes for a moment, hissed and cast swear words. But they were as united on one subject as they were on their aversion to rain, mice and cat boxes: their aversion to their neighbors.

It was a family not unlike their own. Husband, wife, children, from time to time there were visitors. Nevertheless, these people were different. Apart from a few outward appearances, there was one main difference: they were dog owners.

"A really unbearable hoi polloi," he thought to himself, whenever he saw the neighbors. Lenny, too, seemed to share this view, always sat in the garden with his backside facing the neighbor's house and greeted anyone who left it by demonstratively turning his head away slowly, eyes firmly closed.

Both males were only seen next door when they relieved themselves on the lawn there. The fact that the neighbors were always greatly agitated about it only increased the fun. The neighbor then shook his clenched fist as he stormed out of the house and expressed his anger: "Get lost, you stupid critter!" Although he still seemed to be the fastest in the neighboring family, he was far too slow to ever catch one of the tomcats. Running away from the rushing rage, there was even enough time to stop right at the fence and turn around with a scornful look before a cat-typical, vertical leap led to the top of the fence post. A casual jump into the own garden demonstrated superiority once again, because the man had never come within striking distance of one of the tomcats.

Exasperated and panting loudly after the short sprint, the man then usually shouted something along the lines of "Poop in your own yard!"

But why would they do that? They pooped deliberately in the neighbor's yard. "A truly mindless exclamation that only proves how stupid these people are," he thought every time. "It's a pity these people don't have a sandbox, because otherwise I would shit in that."

Lenny seemed to think similarly. "Have fun with the monkeys next door, you dog," Lenny yelled at him when he met him on the way out. Another time it was "Well, go over to your new friends, you coyote," which he countered with "Better a coyote than a puppy dog like you!" Worse insults were avoided to prevent paw-fisticuffs. Once, even a quite jaunty conversation came about.

"Did you relieve yourself pleasantly?" Lenny asked in passing, when the orange one returned from the neighbor's garden.

"Oh yes, Lenny, I did! On the way back you feel so light, the fence could be a foot higher and it would be just as easy to climb!"

"Ha-ha, terrific!" Lenny laughed.

"The neighbors must have thought it was terrific too! After all, they even carry their dog's excrement around in bags. So I thought to myself, I'll leave a gift there."

"Let me guess: They'll have to wrap it themselves?"

"Ha-ha! Fabulous, Lenny, that was a good one!" He had to laugh aloud.

Lenny bent the conversation into a less fecal direction: "What do you hate most about our neighbors?"

"Where do I begin," he said, while sorting his thoughts. "First of all, they're dog owners, which actually says it all. But let me explain: These people voluntarily live with an animal that stinks with every rain shower and has no character of its own. They have chosen a true pet. What does that say about these people?"

"That they need someone hunching in front of them," was Lenny's dry answer.

"Completely correct! And why do they need that? Because they are characterless themselves! They couldn't cope with a tomcat!"

"That is why there are no cat owners, because we do not let ourselves be owned! Only a dog is submissive enough to be tamed, to be owned. A person who needs something like that is no better than the dog itself," Lenny summarized his view of things.

"Right, basically they're all dogs. The whole lot of them. But in this particular case, even their appearance is a disgrace and hardly bearable. They all look alike," he said scornfully.

"You know, they say that dogs and their owners are becoming more and more similar over time. I think that is a lie. I rather believe that a dog person gets exactly the dog he deserves, to whom he fits." Lenny motioned with his head towards the neighboring property. "And those over there probably looked like their dog before they met him for the first time!"

"Good theory! I'm afraid I have to agree with you again ..." he said and disappeared inside. Lenny didn't look after him, but disappeared between the bushes at the edge of the property.

But the tomcats were not alone with their aversion to the neighbors. Their own family also held a grudge against them, which was often the subject of the evening conversations. One evening the topic came up again.

"Did you see that our cat crapped in their backyard?" the daughter asked. "That was hilarious!"

"Both of them have already crapped in their backyard," cried the son.

"We're eating!" the mother called to order.

"But it's really cool, today it happened again! Did you see that guy run out and get upset about the turd. It would have been so funny if he had stepped in it." The son was thrilled.

"We're eating!" The mother repeated.

"For real, I would have wished that the poop had stuck to his shoe and he had to scrape it out," cried the daughter euphorically.

The mother became louder. "We're eating!" But she could not wipe off a grin. "But you're right. I saw it the other day and had to laugh. Serves that creep right."

The son jumped up. "Oh man, that would have been so cool if he had stepped in it! Cat poop stinks so bad. Imagine if he had used his toothbrush to scrape out the sole and later brushed his teeth again with it! Ha-ha, ha-ha!"

"Gross!" cried the daughter.

"Children! We're eating! Enough!"

"Your mother is right. Enough with the cat shit and how cool it is when the neighbor steps in." The father grinned broadly at the mother and gave her a little nudge with his elbow.

"Sweetheart! Now you're starting too!" The mother put her cutlery on the edge of her plate with a loud bang and looked reproachfully around.

Daughter and son could hardly contain themselves and laughed so hard that they had to hold their bellies.

"OK, OK, OK, stop it now, Mom is right," the father brought the unappetizing topic to an end. "I also think it's great that our tomcats don't like these people any more than we do. But maybe we should not provoke them too much. You know how difficult it is with them ..."

The mood suddenly darkened. "Hmm, difficult! That's a very polite way to put it," said the son.

"Exactly! Besides, our tomcats can poop in their backyard as much as they want, if we have to give them money every month," the daughter said.

A conversation developed that the orange tomcat followed attentively. Not that he was interested in the details, or what exactly had happened between the families in the past. Who was to blame for what. Whether an unfortunate chain of misunderstandings between actually well-meaning neighbors was responsible for the bad relationship, or stupidity, carelessness, bad faith or malice. The cat was not interested in how the cycle of word against word could have been broken. Or how everything could have been prevented, if one had only taken a step back at the right time and said "Stop! Let's try to make it this work." If one would have had a change of perspective. An admission of guilt would have been necessary and to move forward like functioning adults.

Or whether the family should have simply made its point of view clear in time and in an unmistakable manner. Defended themselves. Stood up to people who don't want to follow the rules and think they can get away with anything just because you are righteous and honest. These rebellious good-for-nothings, who confuse decency with weakness, should have just been put back into their place in time, and all would have been well.

The tomcat cared very little that the relationship with the neighbors was initially quite good and only gradually deteriorated. That they invited each other to barbecue, lent each other tools or gave each other eggs, onions and flour when there was a shortage. That at some point there were the first disappointments, because some thought they had given more than others, and others thought they were being treated condescendingly. That disappointment turned into quarrel. Controversy about tools returned broken. Fighting about noise and about leaves and about dog shit. Fighting about windows that were smashed by balls, and whether this was intentional or accidental. A fight that escalated one day to such an extent that one neighbor broke the other's nose and is still paying for it.

None of this really interested the cat. But what interested him were two things: First, how he could use the quarrel to get rid of the dog. And, secondly, how in the process he would be able to assert himself as the undisputed number one pet.

Maine Coon

Extensive cuddling and playing had done him good and made him grow further. He surpassed all normal cats in the neighborhood and was now at least as big as the biggest domestic cat: the Maine Coon. He was still playful and cuddly like his cousins. But he wanted to be more, at least a real big cat, or even better, a beast.

However, an inner restlessness prevented his unchecked growth. For two contradictory feelings rumbled inside him: On the one hand, the competition with Lenny triggered an unknown nervousness inside him. On the other hand, he was euphoric about the idea that he could lead his family in a dispute with the neighbors, and perhaps even get rid of the dog, this well-behaved subject.

In order to grow further, he would have to proceed step by step.

11 – April showers

Spring made winter a memory. The days had become longer than the nights, the snow melted, the first crocuses had already passed. Pleasant temperatures led the bees to explore the area. Swarm by swarm, they left their quarters to search for open buds and plunder their pollen. Hyacinths, primroses, heather. Flora and fauna seemed to compete with each other. Soon the garden would be in full bloom.

The light-heartedness of early spring spread to the family, whose condition was exhilarated by the two childish tomcats. Both were playful and showed their best side. Each in his own way.

The orange one had soon evaluated exactly who liked what and tried to be fair to everyone. He let the son hold an object in front of his nose and kept poking at it with his claws extended. A dangerous game, which left many a scratch on the skin. The daughter was made happy by simply letting her tickle him extensively, because she seemed to enjoy his devotion almost more than the tickled one to be tickled. He would wrap himself around the parents' legs, let them feed him, lift him up, or otherwise keep them on their toes, which gave them that feeling of being needed that the almost grown-up children hardly ever gave them anymore.

Lenny acted like the pal who encouraged them to play whenever the family was together. He seemed particularly fond of chasing a ball of wool and throwing it at people with a paw stroke like a tennis racket, only to have it thrown back immediately. Matches lasting minutes, four against one, until exhaustion.

The orange one found such an ingratiation a bit primitive, even similar to doggy retrieving – which Lenny would certainly have either vehemently denied, or described as an appropriate and thus allowed means for the recognition and love of the family. In any case, it only increased the aversion to the black-furred adversary even more. He was annoyed by Lenny. Lenny metaphorically rubbed him the wrong way, like an unobservant person who, not knowing how to touch a cat, tried to stroke him from his tail towards his head. This naughtiness, this prototype of a clumsy approach, caused pretty much the same feeling as the sight of Lenny in the middle of his family: a shake that covered his entire back – but not in the nice way. Not a pleasantly cool tingling sensation. But a tense tremor, somewhere between rage and nausea. Like when hate mixes with stage fright before a big fight.

In the family, however, this seemed to be viewed completely differently. They approached Lenny, laughed and played with him. Both tomcats received a lot of attention and the danger that Lenny would be chosen in the end was real. There was a need for action, because he could by no means let this sloppy con artist pull the wool over their eyes. He relied on a double strategy to get on top in the end. On the one hand, the efforts towards the family had to be further increased, and if necessary successful concepts of the opposite side copied, such as the emphasis on community. On the other hand, he had to tackle his competitor more sharply, weaken him and seek the decisive battle at a favorable opportunity. This asymmetrical approach of agitation and aggression, of flattering and beating, was intended to ensure his triumph and clear the way for him to finally lead the family.

He was confident that his plan would work out. Because the rich supply of affection and food in the last weeks had made sure that he had gained considerable body mass. However, Lenny was also able to feed himself with food and affection, which had made him grow to an imposing size. Like a pocket-sized panther, he roamed silently through the garden, his pitch-black fur standing out threateningly against the colorfulness of the plants. The paws widened to double the size as soon as they were pressed to the ground with swing. With each step, a hump in the fur arose above the straight front leg standing at the ground only to disappear as soon as the opposite leg was loaded. One after the other, the right and left shoulder-blade protruded. Like the mast of a sailing boat lying at anchor tilts from right to left in the swell, the muscular shoulder humps swayed with every step.

Two such characters could not avoid each other forever. Especially within the four walls, dodging became an illusion and living together became increasingly difficult for them. As nice and cheery as the games with the family were, there was a tremendous tension between the two. The moment was always particularly delicate when the two met at the door to the garden, when one's path in and the other's path out surprisingly crossed. When the door was closed, the floor-to-ceiling glazing caused mock fights, threatening gestures and unambiguous hissing. Separated by the pane, they faced each other a few inches apart, their teeth bared so far that the whiskers pointed almost vertically upwards, as if, completing the threat, they wanted to show the enemy the way to heaven.

But when the door was open, the two stood directly in front of each other without a protective wall of glass. His orange fur suddenly lost its shine, settled firmly on his body, became dull and hard. He took a crouched position and held the ground with its far extended claws. As usual, Lenny reacted according to the cat manual with hump and far erected fur. Both males showed the long canines, but for hissing the situation was too serious, the nervousness too great. A whining howl, which started softly and with a deep voice, quickly drowned out all surrounding noises. A harbinger of the imminent escalation.

On several occasions, this situation had turned out diplomatically when it was agreed to maintain the informal non-aggression pact. Cautiously, both had taken a few steps backwards until the yelping gradually ceased and everyone could go their separate ways unharmed. Now, however, one of the two must have moved suddenly, so that they almost touched each other with their noses. They automatically both took a step back and forward again, only to almost collide one more time – like two people trying to pass each other and, right, left, right, running directly towards each other several times.

"Hey!" cried Lenny gruffly on the third miss. "Watch out!"

"You better watch it yourself! Or else something bad will happen here …"

"Is this another one of your empty threats?" Lenny asked.

"You better get out of my way or you'll find out!"

"Get out of your way? You know that this yard ain't big enough for the two of us," Lenny said pompously.

He could not accept such impertinence by the newcomer and instantaneously swiped his claws across Lenny's face. Lenny couldn't parry anymore and yelled up, but in the next moment he went over to the counterattack. The duel quickly escalated. Screams like circular saws could be heard all over the street. The hunting scene began on the terrace, led into the garden and back to the terrace. Chaser became chaser became chaser. Turn on a dime! After him! A completely confusing situation. Paw strokes, claw scratches, bites that missed their target, hit it, bounced off, cut into the flesh. Screams testified to the pain of hits and defensive success. Turning over in the curve and getting up again. To and fro of a conflict between equals.

Past Jonny the hamster, who was holding on to the bars of his cage in great excitement, shaking the bars with all his strength and using all his body weight. It rattled. Nervously he jumped up and down, stretched up in the air to see more. Jonny squeaked like mad: "It's time! The age of cowardice is coming to an end!"

Startled by the noise, the mother came running out. "What's going on here," she called and looked after the cats running around her like lightning. "What's this all about? Hey! Stop it! Stop!"

She needed a moment to adjust her eyes to the high speed of the hunt. The two rushed through the garden and, after one of them turned on a dime, coming straight at her. She tried to separate the two toms by jumping in between them just as they were shooting past her. She made a lunge with one leg and at the same time stretched out her arm jerkily. Her acrobatic dislocation looked like a hockey goalkeeper trying to fend off a puck fired at close range. But while a goalie throws himself well-padded against the round rubber disc, the mother exposed an arm and a leg to the danger of being scratched or bitten.

The collision was to be expected. "Ouch!" cried the mother with a face distorted in pain. It had got her. One of the two had, whether intentionally or accidentally, scratched her, which immediately started to bleed. "You damn varmint! Ah! My leg!"

The mother's sacrifice was in vain, because after a moment of shock the tomcats continued the chase and disappeared behind the corner of the house. The mother first sat down on the floor to deal with the shock.

"What happened here?" said the father as he rushed to his wife on the terrace.

"One of them scratched me! Look, it's even bleeding!" The mother pointed with her head to her hands, with which she pressed on her shin. Between her fingers, a red stain spread across her pants. The fibers of the fabric became visibly saturated with the red liquid.

"Oh God! It hit you full on! There's blood everywhere!" The father was horrified when he saw that even the floorboards of the terrace were smeared with blood.

"Oh, dear!" She carefully took her hands off the wound and compared the bloodstain on her trousers with those on the floor. "That's not mine! It's from the cats!"

"They've got quite a fight," said the father. "I hope they don't kill each other!"

"I tried to prevent that!"

"Never mind. Now come inside. I'll disinfect it quickly!"

While the two disappeared in the house, the fight continued with undiminished severity, shifting several times from one side of the house to the other. Both tomcats landed blows. They bit and scratched each other. Drops of blood covered the ground around the house.

In this struggle, that only the more agile and stronger of the two would be able to decide for himself, the orange fur withstood the majority of the attacks. It pulled itself tight like a second skin, a protective layer. Many hits were cushioned, or slipped off without causing any damage. Nevertheless his blood came out of several wounds. His right ear was torn, a triangular piece missing.

Lenny was also badly hit and had gaping wounds on all extremities, around which his blood-soaked fur stuck to the skin.

No one was willing to give up, and so the chase gradually slowed down, the attacks becoming weaker and more random. Before exhaustion would spread and force a stalemate, suddenly a heavy shower of rain began. Within seconds the two were soaking wet. Light red colored water dripped from their skins into the lawn. And since tomcats hate being soaked with water even more than with their own blood, the fight was over faster than a riot after shooting a water cannon.

12 – Kill switch

He sat on the floor between the sofa and a knee-high pile of irregularly stacked magazines that must have accumulated over a long time. The gap offered him some peace and quiet and protected him from prying eyes. There he could lick his wounds. His protective fur had saved him from worse, but he had gotten several deep scratches in the fight with Lenny, from which still blood seeped. They hurt with every movement. Over and over, he kept licking with his rough tongue over the open wounds in his skin as soon as the escaping blood formed a larger drop. He hastily swallowed the part that stuck to his tongue. The remaining blood on his skin immediately combined with his saliva to form a pink emulsion that dried quickly. It was not long before the blood flow from the wounds dried up and thin, brown crusts formed. Long, overlapping stripes, on whose edges the orange fur stuck, testified to the battle.

"What happened here?" the son asked in bewilderment as he came home from school and saw him sitting in the living room. "The cat has countless scars!"

"They really fought!" said the mother.

The son came closer and examined the condition of the orange cat. "Oh man, the poor guy looks terrible! He's even missing a little corner of his ear!"

"You should see Lenny! He looks even worse. Dad is just upstairs with him."

The son's eyes were peeled open in disbelief. "Has he gotten more? How did that happen?"

"I don't know, I was inside and I just heard the howling on the terrace! I went outside and wanted to intervene. But there was no stopping them." The mother shrugged and pointed to the bandage on her shin. "Look, one even scratched me."

"Whoa," the son put his impressions in one word.

"Yes, it hurt quite a lot. It happened so fast, I didn't even realize who it was."

"Phew! Very dangerous, those two!"

"You said it," said the mother, "but it's not so bad. The tomcats look worse than me. Lenny limps properly."

"And what's Dad doing with him now?" asked the son.

"He looks at the wounds and gives him something to eat and drink."

"I'll go up and have a look," said the son and hurried up the stairs.

Lenny's obviously severe wound was satisfying to the orange tomcat. It nourished the hope of being able to finish Lenny off soon. For the conflict could not be allowed to repeat itself. The danger of being killed was too great. The next blow had to be dealt soon and with the necessary cunning. There was no room for mistakes: a false sense of honor, which might tempt him once again to a fair duel between two rested peers, was out of place. He could no longer afford fair play. Especially since he could only rely on one thing with Lenny: the end of fair play. Would Lenny lure him into an ambush? Hard hit, both had to face another battle skeptically. It was now up to them to be the first to get better and to seek a decision. No matter how.

In the following days the weather remained rainy and even in the best of health there was no way to think of leaving the house as a tomcat. So both stayed indoors during their recovery. The family struggled with changing emotions and discussed at dinner how to proceed with the two.

"It won't go on like this, that's for sure!" The father slammed his hand on the table. "Your mother got a big scratch and I don't want anything worse to happen!"

"That's right! Imagine that they catch you in the eye," the mother agreed. "Besides, the two are too dangerous for each other. One of them will die in the end!"

"And what do you think should happen now?" asked the son.

"Someone has to go," said the mother and looked at the children with a challenging look.

Horrified, the daughter called out, "But we can't turn out a wounded cat!"

"Yes, besides, which one of them do you want to throw out?" asked the son. "They have ripped each other to pieces! We don't even know who started it."

"That doesn't matter! Both of them can't stay, and that's it," said the mother. "We'll wait until they're healthy, but then one of them will have to go!"

The father took her side. "You are right. When they're well again, we'll kick one out." His firm voice left no doubt. In the long run, only one of the two would be able to stay. A lasting coexistence was impossible.

The orange tomcat had heard the conversation and was worried. But since his healing progressed rapidly, he was also confident. He stayed on the first floor and tried to play with the family as much as possible, even in spite of pain. For example, he lay on his back and let each of the four people grab one of his legs and then carry him together through the living room as if he were being transported to the hospital on a stretcher. After he was laid down on the sofa, the family burst into laughter. They also gently stroked his wounds, which improved their blood supply and softened the scabs. It did them good and his wounds healed quickly.

On the other hand, nothing could be seen of Lenny for days before he finally dared to go down the stairs, still limping slightly. He seemed bent. His wounds were still clearly visible and his reserved look was a sign of insecurity. Lenny's healing must have been slower despite caring for him.

Lenny's orange opponent took note of his pain-distorted face with joy. "Well, does it still hurt?" he asked him in the language of the animals.

"A little," Lenny replied. "But I see our draw has left its mark on you as well! You don't look too good! Haven't you recovered properly?"

He smelled this cheap bluff a hundred yards upwind. Lenny's slow recovery was obvious. "A draw? You can't fool me. I can see your pain," he shouted.

"Don't be ridiculous, I'm perfectly fine," said Lenny with a nervous tremor in his voice.

"Perfectly fine. Alright. It seems that your judgement has been damaged as well as your body," he replied, sticking his chest out a little further than usual. "Perhaps you should find another family before I put an end to you!"

"Nonsense! I'm well and I'm craving for blood," Lenny said combatively.

"I'm pessimistic," he replied.

Then Lenny turned around and went back to the second floor. Slowly he climbed each step, one by one. At the top he turned around once more. "Pessimistic?" he asked rhetorically. "Surely you know that the darkest hour is just before the dawn!"

Motionless, the orange tom looked at him from afar. "Wrong. It's always darkest just before the light goes out entirely ..."

The chance was there and he intended to take it. Waiting for Lenny to possibly pick himself up was not an option. Also, waiting for the family to kick either of them out was not an option. That's why he had to take action, and soon.

He remembered what his role model and old companion Monty had told him about dealing with opposition. Monty was not exactly squeamish when it came to putting other animals who wanted to take over his position into their place. No problem for Monty, since he had been conspicuously aggressive since childhood. A fact he was proud of even as an adult tomcat, because he liked to tell about an incident in which he, only a few months old, had seriously injured a kitten of the same age with his scythe-sharp claws. Years later, a tomcat ventured into Monty's family and wanted to take his place. Quickly, he pulled the plug on him. Monti tore his opponent to pieces in front of the family, who were shocked and never considered another pet.

These stories inspired the orange tomcat and he wanted to pull a Monty. Not only killing two birds with one stone, but ripping to pieces and humiliating. Remove the enemy and at the same moment make it clear to the family who the pet is. That moment had come.

And so the following night he crept up to the second floor. It had to be quick and quiet. No one should hear and then interfere. It had to be a sure thing and it was. Hardly a sound, hardly a rustling. Nothing to hear in the darkest hour of the night. Until, with the rising sun, an untiring clattering of the hamster cage woke the first family members. Jonny shook his bars like a dervish.

"Ahhhhhhhhh!!!!!" the daughter screamed into the flat hand in front of her mouth, shaking her head.

At the highest point of the stairs there was a pool of blood on the floor, reaching between the bars of the banister. Falling drops picked up enough speed to hit the small red lake one floor below with a clearly audible splash. Splash, splash. Splash, splash.

13 – Very hard, but very fairly

The daughter's scream had drawn them over. Only a few seconds passed before all the family members appeared on the landing. It took much longer for one of them to produce an orderly sentence. Complete dismay was written all over their faces. They looked incredulously at the pool of blood at their feet.

"What's going on here?" the mother finally asked.

The daughter reacted brusquely: "What do you think? There is blood everywhere!"

"I can see that! But is that your blood?"

"No," replied the daughter calmly, while she showed both sides of her intact hands as if to prove it.

The four looked at each other and touched their own clothes to make sure that no blood was on them. Unbelievingly they shook their heads.

"I don't know where that came from," said the father. "It must be from one of the cats! Did anyone hear anything?"

Again, they all shook their heads silently.

"I think it's Lenny's blood. Because he's completely clean!" The mother pointed to the orange tomcat sitting at the bottom of the stairs, looking at the scene with big eyes, as if he couldn't harm a fly. He carefully licked his paws off. His spotlessly clean fur stood off as if he had been rubbed with a balloon. He looked fluffy and sugar sweet. His satisfied purring could still be heard on the second floor.

"True, it cannot be his blood. But where is Lenny?" the father asked.

"I don't see him," stammered the daughter.

"I don't see a trace of blood either," the son added.

"Lenny?" cried the mother through the house. "Lenny?" But there was no reaction.

"There must be traces of blood leading somewhere with such a massacre," said the son.

"Come on! We'll look for him! He can't be far away," said the mother.

The family walked around for minutes looking for the black cat in every room, in every corner. Under the beds, behind the curtains, in the closets and on the chairs.

"We have to look in the yard, too," said the mother and ran out herself.

"Okay, I'll look in the cellar," said the father.

But Lenny remained missing. They searched everything for him in vain. No body, dead or alive, and no trace of blood that could have led to a body. Nothing.

"I don't believe it," cried the mother finally and put her fists to the side of her hips.

"He's gone," sobbed the daughter. "The poor guy is probably injured."

"If there is no trace of blood and he is no longer here, it can't be that bad," said the son dryly.

The daughter wiped a tear from her eye. "It is surely bad. So bad that he ran away."

"He probably hurt him so badly that he ran away," said the mother, pointing again at the orange cat who was still nursing his paws. "Poor Lenny! Let's hope he's not lying dead out there somewhere."

"If he had bled when he ran away, there would be a trail of blood," the son repeated. "It can't be so bad."

"Maybe it was an accident," said the father cautiously. "It could be, couldn't it? Maybe his wounds opened up again and he ran away in fright. Would explain everything."

"Well! That's a bit far-fetched," the mother contradicted. "I'm sure it was him!"

"But you don't know that! He is totally well-behaved," said

the son. "It was probably like Dad said, and Lenny ran away, because he realized that he is weaker."

"I hope you are right. I think you're right," said the daughter.

"We will never know!" said the father. "Come on, let's clean up this mess."

The daughter and son nodded and got started. "Where is this going to lead us?" murmured the mother to herself. But she could not confirm her suspicions, no clues, no evidence. The orange tomcat slowly closed his big rolling eyes, and looked as satisfied as only cats can.

Meanwhile, Jonny the hamster ran up and down in his cage incessantly, whimpering nervously, "Murderer, murderer," he murmured to himself. "Murderer, murderer," very quietly, again and again.

Annoyed, the orange cat finally turned to the hamster and hissed: "What's your problem? Give it a rest!"

"My problem? You are a murderer! That's my problem!"

"Murderer? That's crazy. If two duel, the winner is not a murderer in the end," said the cat dryly.

"Why couldn't you just get along?" asked the hamster.

"There can only be one cat at the head of a family."

"And now? Do you think you have total authority now?"

"That's the way it's got to be!"

"But you're flat-out wrong! No one has that much authority."

"We'll see."

"Lenny wouldn't have had such fantasies. He was peaceful and wanted only the best for everyone. And you chased him away," said the hamster.

"You're so naive. If Lenny had made it to my place, all good intentions would have gone out the window. It's always like that."

"Lenny was a good guy."

"I'll tell you what Lenny was: shifty! I liked him at some point and I have no objection, except for one thing: he was not a very capable or competent cat," he said. "He bothered me. But shifty Lenny got what he deserved."

"Nobody deserves to go out like that," said Jonny, his shoulders sagging with discouragement.

"You know, I hit him pretty hard, but fairly," he said. "Probably very hard, but very fairly."

That was the end of the matter for the cat. Demonstratively he closed his eyes again and turned his head away.

Lynx

His opponent had been cleared out of the way. He probably could have killed him in the middle of the street, right in front of the house, and he would not have been prosecuted. It was an intoxicating feeling. It felt as if he was unstoppable. Hardly any other animal would dare trying to take this place away from him. A feeling that was better and more intense than any caress or feast could convey. It gave him a tremendous boost.

He felt strong and big like a lynx and looked like one. Not a too big house cat, but a real predator that could tear even dogs to pieces if it wanted to.

14 – Supreme leader

Other animals were no danger anymore. Now he now wanted to finally get the family on his side once and for all. The plan was simple. He had to impress these people! Once again, he wanted to follow his role model Monty and do the incredible: speak. Talk to people. He was determined to learn. He had seen how the simplest messages were enough to make people go crazy and fulfill a tomcat's every wish. This motivated him to practice imitating human sounds from now on.

He had a clear plan and could devote himself to vocal training in the following days and weeks, in peace and quiet. He tirelessly trained his voice, tried to produce deep tones and to direct them into orderly paths. With a small larynx and short vocal chords compared to humans, it was easy to emit high-frequency cries. But complex vibration sequences, as required by the spoken word, were a great challenge. His voice color was also too bright to be taken seriously.

Whenever he was not sleeping, eating or playing, he now trained the flexibility of his voice, tongue and lips. He meowed up and down the whole scale to hit deeper and deeper tones. He bent the tongue to a spoon as if he was drinking and then turned it over. He rotated with a kissing mouth in front of the incisors. The many exercises were exhausting, and so he continually stretched his entire mouth apparatus, with yawning typical of a tomcat: his head laid back on his neck, eyes closed, his mouth opened so wide that all teeth were exposed, his tongue tensed in all directions until it trembled.

He attentively observes the mouth movements of speaking people to recognize and imitate patterns. It took some time, with an endless series of failed attempts, but he gradually made small progress. The first meaningful tone sequences left his mouth and finally came together in simple words. Often his tongue hit his incisors and produced unwanted syllables. Nevertheless, he soon wanted to show what he had learned. He was sure to knock his family off their feet if he would produce a human sentence. Or at least one word. They would be so impressed that they – unlike him – would be speechless.

But that was not yet the case. He trained himself in patience. Practiced. His first utterance should be perfect. His first human meow.

He was full of self-confidence, because he felt good, and felt good for his self-confidence. His progress electrified him. And he grew. By now, he towered above all knees and was too big to wiggle his way between the family's legs. "Stop! No further here! You're too big! You won't fit through here anymore," they said when he almost got stuck between two legs again.

The mood was good, and the day came when he wanted to show his skills. When the whole family wanted to go out together one evening, he took advantage of the situation and set up in front of the door. Everyone already had their jackets in their hands and wanted to leave the house. But they could not get past him. He blocked the exit. The father stroked him briefly over the head as a farewell gesture. "Come on! Let us out. Let's go!"

When the father tried to reach past him for the door handle, the cat opened his mouth and muttered "sssooo sssad!" A slight lisp could not diminish his pride. He spoke, or rather meowed human words!

The casual conversation of the family fell silent immediately. Incredulous, the four people slowly turned around. They looked as if the incarnate had appeared to them. Fascinated, and with ears like rhubarb leaves, they waited for what they heard to be repeated, as if to make sure they were not dreaming.

In all calmness, he let the seconds pass, while the open mouths slowly closed. The son almost looked a little disappointed when he finally asked, "Did you hear that too?" They nodded without taking their eyes off the cat.

"Come on, do it again," demanded the daughter, who could not have guessed that this was a deliberate pause to increase the drama.

He set up a gaze, which – even if this association was far from his mind – could only be described as a dog's gaze. Slowly he opened his mouth, whereupon the amazed people opened theirs. Finally, he released the family from their tension and meowed again, "sssooo sssad!"

Like scoring a last-minute goal, the children pulled their arms up and cheered, hopped, ran towards him, embraced him. The two parents, however, shook their heads suspiciously, as if they refused to believe what they had just experienced, as if they did not trust their senses. But it was true. Their cat spoke to them. Absurd, but undeniable.

"Say something else," cried the daughter.

"Yes, tell me why you are sad," cried the son and shook the cat's shoulder excitedly. "Say something!"

"Stay here," he complained. "So sad."

"Whhaaaattt?" cried the son, "Whoa," said the daughter. Ecstatically, the two repeated their calls and patted the cat, as one usually only does with dogs.

"Unbelievable!" The mother shook her head more and more violently. "Absolutely unbelievable!"

"Did you hear that, darling?" the father asked, knowing full well that his wife had heard every word. "The cat is sad when we leave him alone. I guess we'll have to stay at home now. I don't believe it!" His words were mixed with unbelieving laughter.

"Unbelievable," the mother said once again, without answering her husband's rhetorical question.

The cat's plan had worked out. The children were beside themselves and he had their enthusiasm on his side once again. His tireless voice training paid off. Euphoria and incredulous amazement mixed into a spicy cocktail of feelings, which he intended to slurp out slowly and with relish. He wanted to ride this wave for as long as possible, because with a family that was enthusiastic about him, a lot could be achieved. He would also overcome the mother's obvious skepticism.

"But his voice is a bit croaky, isn't it?" the mother suddenly said.

He deliberately overheard this impudence, but the children could not ignore it.

"Croaky? Mom! Our cat can talk!" cried the daughter.

"You don't get how whack this is, dude!" cried the son.

"I'm not a dude!" The mother raised her right index finger in warning, which was a strange threatening gesture in the eyes of the cat because she was missing claws. But her look pierced the son. "And yes, I get how whack this is!"

"Sweetheart, everything is fine," said the father calmly, smiled benignly and came over to the cat to fluff him through the orange mane in recognition. "You can talk, you fine fellow." The father scratched the cat behind his ears and finally turned to the others. "And if he gets sad when we leave, we'll stay home tonight and hear if he has anything else to tell, right?"

"Yeah," the children shouted happily.

"OK, if you want," added the mother and hung her jacket back on the coat hook. "Well, I'll prepare some nibbles," she said and disappeared into the kitchen.

And so they spent that balmy early summer evening with the windows and doors open in the living room, listening to the cat and laughing a lot together. Although he couldn't put his complex world of thoughts into human words, his practiced plays went down very well. It was a whole new way to communicate – and he loved it!

"Tremendous," he kept muttering. It seemed to be his favorite word.

Suddenly the barking of the neighboring dog sounded, which immediately caused a feeling of aversion and even disgust in him. "Dog is baaad," he complained and could not suppress neither hissing nor snarls.

A resounding laughter filled the room, which was certainly also to be heard by the hated neighbors. The reactions ranged from "You're right," to a meowing back "Oh yes, dog is baaad," which imitated the cat's comical way of speaking.

"Oh man, you're really the greatest cat I've ever seen," said the daughter.

"Really, you are the greatest," added the son. "You really are the greatest cat ever!"

"That's right, we surely still have a lot to expect from you. We'll see what else you learn," said the mother, stroked him briefly and leaned back into the sofa with folded arms.

"That is true! He really is the supreme cat," said the father while cuddling him. "And the dearest cat!"

"Exactly, the biggest, dearest tomcat, with the tiniest paws," said the daughter and stroked him lovingly over the front legs down to the paws, which were actually a bit small for his height.

"Ha-ha-ha," everyone yelled unanimously.

"That's right, I hadn't noticed that yet! Your paws are really quite small," the mother added, which again led to loud laughter.

Surprised by this unexpected insult, he could only mutter "But super-duper claws!"

What an entertaining counterattack. He reaped another laugh. But it was meant quite seriously, because even though he was bad at mental arithmetic, he knew that his claws were many times longer and sharper than the fingernails assembled in this living room.

They thought up more nicknames, played extensively and tried to elicit more words from him. Exuberance made the evening fly by. When, much later than usual, the first yawning noises began to mingle with the conversation, the father closed the merry circle. "Well, I'm beat. I'm going to bed!" The children stayed a while longer, but were also unable to resist the growing tiredness for long. One by one, they left the cat until he lay alone in the living room.

The exuberant mood seemed to make Lenny's disappearance forgotten, which meant that he had reached another interim goal: He was on top, the undisputed pet and true head of the family. He was satisfied. And he could feel how he continued to grow.

An exciting evening came to an end. As tired as he was, he could have fallen asleep immediately. Only the thing with the little paws kept him awake for a while. Had these people already forgotten what these paws could do? It was the downer of this otherwise perfect day. Until he finally disappeared into the realm of dreams, his thoughts circled around it several times: "Look at these paws! Are they small? They're not small! Look at these paws! Are they small? They're not small!"

15 – They're laughing at us

His wounds had long since healed and now that the weather had finally improved, he enjoyed roaming the garden again. His path led him across the lawn and under the trees to the rose bushes, which were in their full splendor this time of year. There he lingered for a moment, extensively smelled the blossoms, and walked on. He liked to stroll around and was proud to be the number one tomcat in this beautiful corner of the earth. He passed the vegetable patch without being interested in its fruits and went back to the house, where his orange coat stood out in front of the white paint. There he sat down in front of the terrace, let the sun shine in his face and held court.

One after the other, all members of the family came to check on his well-being, to play with him a little, and of course to see if he would say something again. They were thrilled every time he meowed a new short phrase. Sometimes he even answered direct questions.

"Well how are you today?" asked the daughter and ran him gently over his paws.

"Grrrreat," he replied through his teeth.

"Grrrreat? That's good." The daughter laughed and shook his muscular shoulder in a friendly manner. "Wow, you are really strong! A really stable guy!"

"Sss-stable!" he repeated.

"Yes! You are stable!"

"Sss-super sss-stable!"

Now the daughter laughed even louder. "Oh, this is so funny! You are really babbling! You're so smart," she called to him and winked.

"Sss-smart," he hissed.

"Yes, a little genius," she said.

"Sss-stable genius," he purred back. He liked the thought,

because that was exactly how he saw himself: unwavering and intelligent.

"A stable genius?" The daughter had to grin broadly, for she was obviously amused by this comical statement. "Yes, you are! A talking cat is always a stable genius." Then the daughter stood up, looked at him in love and disappeared blissfully into the house.

The daughter was followed by the son, who paid a visit to his favorite tomcat to stroke him extensively. Between the eyes, the circular touches and gentle pressure were most pleasant. The son showed great perseverance, and finally elicited the hoped-for appreciation from him.

Purrrrrrrr. "Good boy," he slowly muttered to the son, keeping his eyes closed. Purrrrrrrr! What a treat! As head of the family, he lived it up. If it were absolutely necessary, he would be able to bear this petting for hours. Purrrrrrr. "Good boy," he kept muttering.

Every time he said these two words, the son stroked a little faster. The appreciation of his efforts seemed to motivate him. When the stroke frequency then gradually decreased, a slow "Good boy" from the cat was enough to remind the son of the right speed again. Whether the son did this purposely to make the cat talk remained his secret. Finally, however, he stood up and left the tomcat. "I must go! homework. See you later! But here comes Daddy. He'll keep stroking you."

The baton was passed on to the father. However, he showed less endurance in caressing the cat than the children. "Well, are you enjoying the sun?" he asked the cat rhetorically, who obviously enjoyed the sun's rays on his fur so much that he made himself as long as he could to catch more of them. "Can I get you anything?" the father asked, without expecting a concrete answer.

"Meeeeeeat," replied the cat. "Fresh-sssh!"

Then the father made huge eyes and came a little bit closer with his head, as if he had not understood the cat properly. "Meat?" he asked quietly? "You want meat?"

He reluctantly repeated: "Meeeat!"

Then the father jumped up and ran hastily into the house. "Sweetheart, do we have any meat? The cat wants meat! Dear?"

"The cat asked for it?" The mother was breathing heavily as she climbed up the basement stairs with a heavy laundry basket in her hands, while her husband nodded his head. "Well, yes, in the fridge!"

"Can you give him something?" the father asked in a quick voice.

"If I have to. And if you hang this up," said the mother, as she firmly pressed the heavy basket with the still wet laundry into her husband's hands, as if to convey to him that the housework doesn't do itself.

"Sure!"

"But next time it's your turn to feed him," she said quietly.

"Sure," he said, and went lightly whistling to the clothesline hanging behind the house.

With a fist-sized snack of ground beef, the mother hurried to meet the waiting tomcat, who gladly accepted it on a small, silver-plated tray. "Here you go," she said and carefully took a step back.

She watched the cat and how he choked down the soft lumps of meat. She was disgusted by the sight of the minced meat protruding between his teeth and the way he caught the falling lumps with snapping jaws. "Why is everyone so thrilled about you?" she whispered half to him, half to herself. The plate was emptied in no time at all, and he demanded a second helping of "Morrrre!"

She stood up to fulfill his wish and shook her head. "Oh dear, you'll eat the hair off our heads," she said and made her way to the kitchen. She hurriedly returned with another portion of meat. "Here you go again," she said, while he immediately began to gobble. "If you continue to eat so much, you will never stop growing, you glutton!" How right she was, she could not yet guess.

He bathed in the admiration that surrounded him since his first meowed word. It gave him a lift and accelerated his growth process, which was not exactly detrimental to his pride. He felt good and was completely with himself. Just as the sun warmed his chest from outside, contentment warmed it from inside. He enjoyed being himself, and if he had ever had self-doubt, it was gone now. There was no longer any need for a camouflage. Rather, the orange color of his fur gave the green vegetation around him a striking spot of color. The cat was the decorative element of that garden. He enjoyed his place in the sun and used the peace and quiet to reflect.

"It may be good to possess power that rests on claws. But isn't it better and more satisfying to win the heart of a family?" he thought. Had his undisputed, even incontestable position made him lenient? He let his gaze glide over his territory. He was calm as could be.

Suddenly this idyll was disturbed by dog barking from the neighbor's garden. A circumstance that went so violently against his grain that it could hardly be worse – figuratively and literally. He was actually torn from his daydreams of omnipotence by this wretched mutt! "Intolerable, this yapping amoeba! I didn't even know that there were unicellular organisms with four legs," he thought, while his tail was seized by a restless waving and swung like a whip from side to side.

It did not hold him in place for long. Suddenly he jumped up and ran to the fence. A short, loud roar, which had little in common with the cute scratching and hissing sound normal house cats give off during a tantrum, provided silence. It was a respectable noise. Somewhere between the roar of a lion in heat and an approaching express train. The dog was surprised and gave in quickly. Although he looked like a cross between a Doberman and a Newfoundlander – proud and strong – he ran away with his tail between his legs.

"Dummy dog," he meowed when the son, startled by the noise, hurried to him.

"Yes, the dog's a dummy," he tried to calm him down.

But talking him down and patting his head could not relieve his tension. He wanted to see action. "Do something," was the cat's answer.

"Oh, what shall we do? Hmm? You?" said the son.

The cat did not feel taken seriously. "Get it done," he meowed. "Fast."

"We'll think of something, OK?"

When the neighbor suddenly appeared at the fence, the son took the opportunity to speak to him. "Tell me, is the barking necessary? Our cat is getting restless."

"Well, if your cat doesn't like it, I'll explain it to my dog." The neighbor grinned disparagingly. His disregard for the son's wish was obvious.

"I'm serious! Forbid the dog to bark. He always does what you say anyway."

"Why should I do that? He was only barking. It's perfectly normal. He's a dog!" said the neighbor. "But your weird giant cat scared him away! Maybe you'll forbid your fat furball to hiss."

The son ran red with anger. "He wouldn't do that if your mutt wouldn't bark all the time. Make sure that this noise stops!" he shouted.

"What if it doesn't?" asked the neighbor.

"Maybe I'll come over and sort it out myself," the son threatened.

"That's right, you'll sort it out! I dare you to ..." The neighbor waved away, turned around and laughed out loud.

"You will see! I'm serious!" the son shouted after the neighbor.

The neighbor stopped for a moment and said calmly: "You'll

handle this? Go ahead and try. But don't be surprised if I kick your ass!" He shook his head and laughed as he went back into the house.

"I mean it," the son murmured after him a few more times.

This neighborhood quarrel was just what the cat wanted. It was only an announcement, but at least it was a step in the right direction. The tail wagging became slower. In peace he could dream the rest of the afternoon.

During the evening meal, which took place on the terrace on most of these mild early summer days, the family came to talk about the tomcat, who sat right next to the table and enjoyed a delicious meat pot. He became attentive when the incident with the neighbor's dog was mentioned.

"The two don't like each other very much," the mother remarked. "When the dog barks, the cat goes wild!"

"That's right, he got really angry today and hissed around. I have never heard anything like that before," said the daughter.

"Why does he hate the dog so much?" asked the father, who obviously hadn't noticed the scene.

"I think he not only hates the dog. He also hates the neighbors. He has also hissed at them," the daughter said.

"That's good! You can only hate these idiots." The son raised his fist and looked at the cat. "You did a good job! Keep up the good work!" The cat acknowledged the speech with a gentle nod, without looking up from his bowl.

"I'd rather not. If he continues like this, they will get scared," said the mother.

"That's what I said: well done," cried the son and greeted the cat with his fist once more. Again he nodded benevolently.

"Not that there is any more trouble, I'm just saying," added the mother. "Maybe they will call the police. Not that they take your cat from you."

The son remained combative: "If there is trouble, that's fine with me! I can't stand these people. I'm not afraid of them."

"Relax, son," the father cut him off. "Nothing has happened yet except a little barking. We will not be provoked."

"That's right, we'll wait," added the mother. "We don't want to fight with them. We don't care about the neighbors."

"No!" cried the son as he rose and hit the table with his flat hand. "We do care, because he laughed at me. The guy laughed at me!" After a moment, he slowly sat back down. "They're laughing at us!"

Then the cat lifted his head for the first time that evening and meowed: "They're laughing at us!"

Leopard

The long hours of practice had paid off. He meowed human words and became more and more adept at using his voice. His expression became more nuanced and he hardly ever lisped. He realized how powerful this vocal instrument was for him, because he reached his family directly and only filtered through his own limitations. What if he could also put more complex thoughts into short formulas? His possibilities would be enormous! For this he had to train his voice further.

The enthusiasm of his family and the prospect of more, gave him a boost. By now he was as big as a leopard, and he continued to grow.

16 – The little man

"So, you're enjoying your fame?" Jonny asked the cat in the language of the animals.

"Fame? I am not a musician after all. I am not famous. I am revered," he replied dryly, while chewing a fillet of beef, looking down from above into Jonny's cage.

The hamster held on to the roof of his wooden house with one hand and raised the other, clenched into a tiny fist. "Spare me your sophistry, you elitist snot! I don't care about fame or veneration!"

"Okay, so semantic niceties are not your problem. Then what is your problem?" he asked.

"They make your every wish come true, while there is nothing left for me. I get water and bread crumbs. And only on the good days!"

"You don't look like you're getting too little to eat. Your corpulence is enormous for a tiny creature like you," he replied, still chewing.

An angry blush shone through Jonny's fur. "You out of touch, fat cat! You don't know what it's like in a cage like this! Ever since everyone here has been dancing to your tune, I'm hardly ever taken in hand, not stroked anymore! I'm not even allowed in the backyard since you've been there!"

"I find the attention you receive entirely appropriate."

"Insolence!" cried Jonny in rage. "What impertinence, that someone like you should say such things! Someone who has everything! All you have to do is purr for a moment and someone will come and pamper you immediately. And what do I get?"

"You know, my dear Jonny, privileges are earned."

"Earn? I don't think I can hear you. How is a little hamster like me supposed to earn what you were born with?"

"Life isn't fair."

"So you admit you're a con artist. From day one on the winning streak, while people like me have to deal with what we get," the hamster cried angrily.

"What do you want from me?" he asked calmly.

Jonny climbed up a few rungs of the cage grate. He shook the bars violently, and they began to rattle loudly. "Freedom! Out of the hamster wheel, out of the cage!"

"Be glad you're in there. At least it's safe. If you were out here, you would immediately run for a hole in the ground," he said.

"Yes, because of people like you! Predators that will tear us apart if we venture too far out. But I will be free and never submit. We hamsters will rise one day!" Jonny could not be calmed, his head was glowing.

"First of all, tiny creatures like you always claim to rise, and then they just lie in the sawdust. And second, you forgot something very important! I am the one who patrols the fence. I keep the yard clean and keep the neighbor's dog from coming to us. Without me, the mutt would make himself at home here. And what's more, everything would be full of birds of prey. The dog would never catch them!" With his broad head, he came very close to the grating, raising the claws of his right paw as a warning. His breath made Jonny's fur flutter and he spoke in a low voice: "Don't think that you would be better off without me! The dog, or any other cat, would take my place. Little animals like you are never really free!"

Then the hamster fell silent. Had he understood the hopelessness of his situation?

The cat looked him firmly in the eyes for a few seconds before he turned around to go into the garden. Just before he reached the door, he stopped once more and gave Jonny an unmistakable advice: "Be good," he said and went outside.

17 – Skirmish

Arriving in the garden, he looked for the most beautiful spot and waited to be served. Now that the sun was at its zenith, he preferred a shady spot near the tree trunk and had cold milk and fresh meat brought directly from the refrigerator. He preferred to enjoy lukewarm milk and snacks towards the evening, when the last rays of sunshine warmed his full belly. He didn't even have to ask for his favorite foods anymore, because his preferences were known. Should something unpleasant end up in his bowl, he simply let it be and soon got a replacement.

It was the same with the obligatory caresses, since he was given at least one brief scratch, pat or smooch at every opportunity, no matter how small. There was still time for that even when a family member just passed him by. For extensive massages, a purr and presenting the body part intended for it, usually the stomach or the underside of his chin, was sufficient. But his preferred places to be scratched were known anyway, as was the preferred way to be scratched. Not too tight, slowly back and forth. Hardly ever did he have to give a hint.

However, the matter-of-fact manner in which his wishes were fulfilled, almost without his intervention, also led to a steady increase in his demands. The more he received, the more he desired, which led to the fact that gifts, which only a short while ago conveyed a feeling of satisfaction and fulfillment, today were already perceived as ordinary. He quickly became accustomed to comfort and soon wanted even greater gifts. The giving hands could not be industrious enough. Hardly a piece of meat was tasty and hardly a stroke was devoted enough. And while the family tried to satisfy him, he grew and grew.

His need to express his deep dislike for the neighbors and their dog also grew. And since no family member spoke back to him, he lived out this need more and more unrestrainedly. He used the afternoon rest to think up new meows for his listeners. The children were on the way, parents nowhere to be seen, and so he had the leisure to ponder which insult he could let loose next. Suddenly the barking of the neighboring dog tore him out of concentration.

As usual, he answered the barking with a hissing, but instead of silence, he only got more barking in response. The argument escalated quickly until the two of them stood face to face, both on their hind legs, with their front paws leaning against the fence, scratching, threatening. Growling, barking and hissing alternated in quick succession. Apparently the dog's pride was injured and he did not want to give in anymore. The dog tried to make up for his obvious inferiority with all the more noise.

A huge ruckus was heard at the boundary of the property, which quickly got the neighbor's attention, rushing into the backyard with a water hose in his hands, ready to separate the opponents. Without any warning, he turned the nozzle completely open and aimed straight for the cat. The firm jet penetrated the fur and soaked the tomcat up to the skin. He saw himself forced to a tactical retreat. With three or four big leaps he was out of reach of the hose and collected himself.

He had been caught on the wrong foot. He sat there crouched and suspiciously focused on the neighbor who turned off the hose and strolled back into the house with the dog. "Kudos," he thought to himself. "This round goes to you. But this battle will not decide the war." The enemy had taken him by surprise. He would turn the tables on him if the opportunity arose.

While his fur dried quickly in the afternoon sun, his anger continued into the evening. It was only the evening conversation that brought him relief, when the family sat in the living room talking about the neighbor's provocation.

"You didn't even notice that your cat was soaked with a hose today, did you?" asked the mother and pointed with a movement of her head to the animal lying in the hallway. "That's probably why he is so quiet today."

"Excuse me?" cried the son in indignation. "Soaked?" said the daughter.

"Yes, the neighbor sprayed him with his garden hose this afternoon."

"And what did you do?" asked the son.

"Nothing, what should I have done? I didn't take the dog barking seriously. Only when it didn't stop, did I look out of the window. But the neighbor had already thrown down his hose and left."

"And the cat?" asked the daughter.

"He ran into the corner and lay in the sun. No big deal."

"That's an effin big deal!" said the son.

The daughter agreed. "Next time, I'll hose *him* down!"

The son grinned. "Do that!"

"Yes, we can't put up with that," said the father. "That's going too far. You should have said something."

"It was already over when I saw it. But you're right. Maybe I'll say something next time," the mother agreed.

"I don't really want to wait for a next time. I'll say something when I see him," said the father.

The conversation developed in the right direction, found the cat, who came to the table and threw in a meow: "They're evil."

"Yes, they're evil. You're right," said the father, while lightly patting the cat on the head.

"Total fool," he continued. "Incompetent."

"Incompetent? Wow, you can say better and better words," said the mother.

"The best words," he meowed calmly.

The father had to grin and continued "That's true. They really are incompetent."

"Say something else," shouted the son to the cat. "What do you think of the neighbors?"

"Total disaster," he meowed.

Everyone laughed, half proud and half amused by his choice of words. For a short moment, the anger about the neighbor was forgotten.

"Worst ever!" he meowed.

"Ha-ha-ha, you're right as usual," laughed the father. "Tell us what you hate most about the neighbor!"

"Fat-ass!" he complained. "Ugly!"

"You're right!" cried the son. "Look at their noses! These people all look like their dog! It's pathetic!"

"Well, well, well," the mother intervened and raised her voice. "Now let's not exaggerate!"

"That's right," replied the daughter. "They all have the same ugly nose. Yuck!"

"Yeah! They look like some overbred boxer," said the son and laughed.

"Come on, guys," said the mother, shocked, while the people she addressed laughed louder and louder.

"Well, dear. People say that dogs and their owners look more and more alike with time," said the father.

"Ha! I rather think they chose each other because they were all equally ugly from the get-go," said the son.

"Let's not get carried away here," said the mother seriously. "None of us likes these people, but we shouldn't sink to that level. Please!"

"They're a pain in the ass and someone needs to hose these guys down!" said the daughter.

"We won't do that," said the mother. "Do you think it'll get better if we pay them back?"

"Absolutely," the cat meowed slowly, before anyone else could answer the question. "Fix it!"

The mother demonstratively didn't look at the cat and shouted: "That won't help. It'll only escalate."

"I want to get back at them. I don't care if it escalates," cried the son. "The cat is right. They're scum."

"Terrible," the cat added looking directly at the mother.

She continued to avoid his gaze. "Well, it wasn't that bad!"

That was enough. A short but loud roar silenced the round. Without averting his gaze from the mother, he finally meowed: "I always get even."

18 – Loosen up

As so often, the cat sat on the step of the terrace and looked contentedly over his garden kingdom, when suddenly grey clouds darkened the sky. The earthy scent of raindrops falling on dry ground could not yet be sensed, but a summer thunderstorm seemed imminent. The wind freshened up and rummaged through the cat's fur in ever stronger gusts so that the underlying skin flashed out. He began to freeze, and so he preferred to exchange his place outside for one inside the house.

Once inside, he positioned himself in a place that every tomcat likes. In the corridor, exactly halfway between the kitchen and the living room, he was right in the middle of it all and enjoyed an excellent view of everything going on in the house. He had the doors to the street, backyard and cellar in view as well as the stairs to the upper floor. No one could enter or leave the house without his knowledge, or even quickly get a beer and go back to the TV. You always had to get past him. Moreover, people had the advantage of short distances in case they wanted to stroke him or bring him something to eat. For those who wanted to pass him, he left a well-measured gap of several inches between his paws and the walls on either side of the corridor. He could no longer lie crosswise in the frame of the kitchen door as he used to. He had become too big in the meantime. But here in the corridor there was enough room for everyone to walk past him comfortably.

"You're in the way! As always," grumbled the mother as she took a big step over his hind legs on her way to the kitchen, leaning against the wall with one hand.

"Excuse me?" he thought to himself. "There's plenty of room here!"

No petting and not a kind word. Instead, criticism. He hadn't had to listen to such pointed remarks from neither the father, nor from the children. But although these groundless accusations annoyed him, they were hardly to be taken seriously. So he decided to let the mother grumble and not to bother about it any further.

"Pet me," he muttered provocatively after her, turned on his back and lifted his front legs to present the spot to be stroked. A body posture that usually did not miss its intention.

"No time," she replied coolly and climbed over him once more in the opposite direction. This time a little more awkward, as she was carrying a tray of dishes in her hands and could hence not support herself against the wall. While she was balancing over his comfortably stretched legs, her lid blew. "You can't lie here," she cried, turned around and tried in vain to push the big, heavy cat away with her foot. She almost lost her balance and could only barely keep her tray from falling. Obviously frustrated by her failure, she became loud. "I need my space here! Go away! Some day I'll stumble over you!"

He remained composed in the expectation that she would calm down again and did nothing. But the mother put the tray on the dining table and came back to him. She got down on her knees and slowly pushed the cat towards the living room with both hands, using her entire body weight. "Get out of the way right now! I want to be able to move freely in my house," she shouted. While he wondered whether her head was turning red from the anger or the physical exertion, he slowly and without any action on his part slid over the smooth tiled floor.

The little woman actually pushed him aside. "An outrageous act," he thought to himself. To simply push a proud cat away like that was unprecedented. No devout Hindu would push a cow aside. But with a tomcat you can do that? "Just you wait," he thought to himself. "Just you wait."

But he was too lazy and too tired today to get seriously upset. He accepted the situation stoically, stayed in place and closed his eyes. The shoving and tugging of the mother was very disturbing. But he wanted to do it like his brethren in the African savannah, who, if they were full, simply loitered around in peace, no matter what was happening around them. He quickly drifted off into his dream world.

The tomcat could not measure if he spent minutes or hours in the arms of Morpheus. But suddenly the noise of a lively conversation catapulted him back into consciousness. He was awake. And in a bad mood. He was reluctant to be woken up by human noise, but the subject made him feel even more uneasy, because it was all about him. Not, as usual, in the form of expressions of esteem and sympathy. It was about his ostensible misconduct.

"The tomcat is taking up more and more space! He is always in the way," the mother complained.

"But that's normal, Mom!" said the son. "Every cat needs its space."

"Yes, but I think ours is particularly bad. He even lies in bed and needs more room there every night."

"But he cycles through the beds," said the daughter. "He's with you only now and then."

"Yes," said the mother, "but when he does, he gets it all for himself. All I have left is the edge of the mattress. And then he lies down on the blanket, too, and I can't pull it out from under him."

Daughter and son smiled at each other.

"That's the same with you, isn't it? Doesn't that bother you?" asked the mother.

"Sure. But that's really cute! When he kicks his nest and then lies down," said the daughter.

"You think it's cute that he's taking your space?"

"What does it matter?" said the son. "He just shows that he likes us. And we like him."

"That's right, he can come to bed whenever he wants," the daughter agreed.

Mother whispered loudly. "But he is everywhere! In the hallway, on the sofa, on the terrace. He is everywhere. He watches every step! Damn it: He talks to us! This is beginning to bother me. You can't do anything anymore if it's not right for him! One must always be considerate of him." She took a deep breath. "He's getting bigger and bigger. He's dangerous and I don't dare say anything more."

"Mom, are you afraid?" asked the son and pushed his eyebrows against each other in disbelief.

"Well, I don't want to be bitten."

"He is here to protect us, Mom," said the daughter. "Only if you treat him unjustly will he become angry."

The mother replied quickly and an octave higher, "Oh, you mean if you don't pet him, if that's what he wants? Or if one does not bring him food when he wants it?"

The son swiftly answered. "That's exactly it, Mom! How could you refuse his wishes? He's even saying them out loud!"

"You're right. That's just it," said the mother. "He talks to us. That's not normal!"

"True, it's cool A-F!" and "Yeah," the kids interjected.

"But *what* he's saying isn't cool," replied the mother. "When he meows, it's either demands or hate! Caress me! Give me food! But I don't want to be bossed around by my cat! Say something, sweetheart!"

"Come on. He has earned that little bit of luxury," said the father with a wink.

"Whatever! But the picking on the neighbors goes too far."

"But they really are terrible," cried the son.

"Yes, they hosed him down," added the daughter.

"Maybe. But that dog-hate is too much," the mother made them consider.

The son raised his fist. "No way! That mutt deserves to get hosed down!"

"Yeah, do it," cried the daughter.

Then the mother whispered even louder. "That's exactly what I don't want. No more conflict!"

"Besides," the father added, with his head stretched far forward and in a low voice, "it doesn't help at all to spray the dog wet, because he doesn't mind that at all! On the contrary – dogs love water. He'd try to catch the water with his mouth."

"Then we'll spray him with mustard or throw rotten eggs," the son said just as quietly.

"Great!" the mother said. "Now you're giving him ideas like that. Thanks!"

"Nothing will happen," the father tried to calm his wife.

"And if it does? If our son throws eggs at the dog, that'll drive the neighbor wild!"

"And then we'll see who gets the ass-kicking!" the son said in a fierce voice.

"No, we won't see that," said the mother. "You don't do anything with the neighbors or their dog. Is that clear?"

Since the children answered only with silenced glances, she continued. "And now we'll start educating our tomcat! He should listen to us and not the other way around."

The cat had heard enough. He opened his eyes, got up and set up next to the table around which the family was gathered. He slowly looked around and stared at everyone just before he slowly meowed clearly and without any lisping. "These nut jobs. I'll take care of them."

"You don't!" The mother hit the table with her fist. "You want to turn us against them!"

"Total hoax," he meowed. "You're lying."

Then the mother ran to the back door, opened it and pointed toward the lawn, which was soaked through with heavy rain showers. "You go out now and stay there. You are not coming to bed and you are not allowed on the sofa anymore! Go on, get out," she ordered, and stretched her finger further in the direction the cat should go.

But he didn't do that. Disobeying the order, he walked slowly across the living room, looking the mother firmly in the eye. Without turning his eyes away from her, he found his way to the carpet, which was in the middle between the dining table and the TV corner. His velvety paws did not make the slightest noise, and you could have heard a pin drop if it hadn't been for the excited breathing of the mother, who stood at the door with trembling lips, infuriated, still pointing her finger outside.

There he stood, between the mother and her family, in the middle of the carpet, in whose soft pile his paws penetrated deeply. He looked the mother right into her face, then turned his head slowly to the rest of the family and then back to the mother. No one said a word. The seconds dragged on.

While the tomcat and mother stood opposite each other like in a duel at noon, he lifted his tail in slow motion, held it up very calmly, and only moved the tip slowly back and forth. His grimace stiffened, and he suddenly let his urine rain down on the carpet in a high arch. It seemed as if he had suppressed his urge to urinate for days. Enormous amounts poured out over the absorbent floor covering, on which a dark coloring spread out in a circle and inexorably strove toward the edge. Once there, the fringes were filled with the yellow liquid and looked like countless small thermometers in which the mercury rose.

The acrid smell of ammonia crept into the noses. He enjoyed how the people, one after the other, twisted their faces in disgust, but nobody dared to say anything. The daughter struggled with her gag reflex, and the mother looked at the event, completely appalled.

Suddenly, the cat jumped at the mother. The huge leap made the ground beneath him tremble. He built himself up directly in front of her and braced his front legs firmly into the ground, so that only a couple of inches separated his head from her chin. His sharp teeth flashed out from under his upper lip. "You are so negative," he complained, "I can't watch it!"

Her mouth trembled, but remained silent. The fear in her eyes was a refreshment for his mind.

"Loosen up and have some fun," he meowed.

After a well-considered pause, he slammed his jaws so hard together that his teeth cracked loudly. Then he lay down on the sofa, which he took up almost completely by now, and closed his eyes contentedly. The penetrating smell would remind everyone of this moment for days.

Cougar

The fact that he was hosed down was forgotten. Disagreements in the family could not harm him either. If there ever was one, the short period of stagnation was over. He felt how he had grown overnight. The mother's scared look had made him sleep well and woke him up full of confidence. His strength was no longer based on affection alone. Respect had been added and now also fear.

He was as big and strong as a cougar. It felt good and he wanted more.

19 – They're fake

The garden had dried up overnight. The excess water had seeped into the ground or been absorbed by the plants, which now, filled with new strength, stretched out towards the rising sun. The morning was pleasantly cool and the fresh air transported the scent of nature particularly well. It was an ideal time to spend the day outdoors, to let body and soul be activated by the first sunrays. The tomcat took advantage of this temporary special offer by the elements and intoxicated himself with his own vitality on a long walk through his territory.

Especially since in this warm summer, every noon the sultriness crept inexorably into every corner of the garden. It laid the veil of lethargy over all living things. Then, at the latest, it was time to retreat into the house for a few hours, where it was shady and a pleasant breeze blew through the wide open doors.

After lying around for hours, he might have felt like stretching his legs or maybe catching a mouse or two. But it was too warm and so he preferred to be served, which, since he had left his mark on the living room carpet, worked even better than before. If almost every wish had been fulfilled hurriedly before, people now seemed to be anxious not to let any wishes arise at all. Perhaps fearing that if they were not fulfilled, they would provoke his displeasure.

Correspondingly dutiful, the daughter came to him at the warmest hour of the day and held a cat brush in her hand, ready to free him from the remains of his undercoat.

"May I brush you?" she asked the cat, who was not indisposed.

Was that supposed to be a joke? "You are great," he muttered, "enormous," and lay on his back stretched out in front of her. With great perseverance, she combed the big animal from head to tail and removed one tuft of hair after the other.

His fur became perceptibly lighter and more airy, which was a benefit on this hot day. Without the help of the industrious girl, it would have taken hours to achieve a similar result with his rough tongue. Besides, he was spared the unpleasant feeling of a mouth full of hair, as well as the undignified sight of a tomcat choking on a fur ball, which did not fit so well to his self-image. It was much more pleasant, and more appropriate, to have someone else do it for him. He was in good spirits. Also, about how the afternoon went on.

They regularly inquired about his well-being. The mother put water out for him without being asked, even flavored with catnip, but avoided getting too close. Shy and bent over, she hastily refilled his bowl and then put the carafe of mint water back into the refrigerator so that it did not lose its temperature. He enjoyed looking her straight in the face and watching her turn away as their eyes crossed. She apparently seemed to want to keep him happy and avoid another confrontation.

The evening walk was cancelled, because the father had bought a present, which gave the cat the greatest joy. Just as he was about to leave the house, there suddenly stood a new scratching post to replace its worn predecessor. The new device was huge and finally fitted his height again. It reached up to just below the ceiling and consisted of different kinds of wood, some of which were covered with pieces of carpet to ensure a varied scratching pleasure. When it got a little cooler in the evening, the cat worked himself to death on it until he had to lie down on the couch exhausted. His claws must have become very sharp.

When he saw how tired the four-legged friend was, the son came into the living room to cuddle with him. "You look worn out! Did you enjoy your new cat tree?" he asked.

"Totally," he muttered quietly.

"Should I turn on the TV for you? Then you can relax."

He nodded and muttered in a weak voice. "No news. They got no clue!"

"Okay, let's see what's coming!" said the son and grabbed the remote control. He zapped through the evening's program, which was as pathetic as ever. He could have been digging through a mud pit and probably wouldn't have gotten any less dirt. It took him quite a while to select all the channels once, only to start all over with little excitement when he reached the end of the list. "Oh man, I think there's nothing but junk on," said the son, resignedly pulling up one of the corners of his mouth and continuing to type hectically on the remote control.

The cat tried to follow the young man's high surfing speed. "There," he moaned.

"What? Teleshopping?" the son asked incredulously.

"Before," he moaned impatiently. "Switch back!"

"Ah! A nature film! That suits you," said the son and grinned affectionately. "I won't turn it up so loud. Then you can sleep better."

"This baby face is just as clueless as the people on the television," he thought to himself. Because the most interesting program in a long time was on and not just any animal film. No documentary about mating beetles in northern South Dakota or Saskatchewan's slowest snails. This show was about lions! Lions rushing their victims to exhaustion in the savannah, ripping them to pieces and then watching with relish as the hyenas fight over the sparse remains. Wonderful! People might prefer to watch documentaries about dictators and wars of days gone by to get a fright or to draw conclusions for their own reality. The orange cat, on the other hand, recognized himself in the sublime kings of the animals. He wanted to learn from them, to measure himself against them.

He was fascinated by the way that the lions sneaked up on their prey, taking them by surprise. They crawl very close in the half-height grass and then strike like lightning. The end follows immediately or after a short chase, but is cruel in any case. Particularly when gnus, zebras and gazelles get their offspring, a banquet lines up to the next. Hunting enthusiasts don't come up short then. None of the peaceful grazers has a chance, that goes beyond an immediate escape-attempt, and even such often end deadly. Usually, only the sacrificial role remains for those chosen by the pack.

"You are really brilliant," he thought. The dominance of the lions paired with the nonchalance of their expansive idleness impressed the cat. Oh, how he too would love to lie under an umbrella thorn acacia with a bloodstained mouth and let his gaze wander contentedly into the distance.

Dreamily he looked at the wild creatures and thought to himself, "I would like to experience such a hunt just once with my old pal Monty! That would be something. Nobody could hold a candle to us and we would make prey as we pleased!" His eyes fell through the glass door to the garden. "Of course, on this ridiculously small property, this wouldn't work!"

As the focus of his eyes readjusted when he looked through the glass door, he recognized his reflection. Unlike normal cats, who are reluctant to look in the mirror, he loved to look at his face, especially now that he recognized his resemblance to the lions on television, and was sure to soon reach their size as well. He had grown month after month. But it was not only abundant meat, not only the affection of the people that made him grow, but also their respect and lately fear. To profit from the timidity of others – a great feeling!

"I am brilliant. Like a lion," he murmured softly to himself. "Huge IQ. Phenomenal mane."

Less than of himself and the lions, he was enthusiastic about the hyenas. They were an unworthy species to him in every respect. Had he not known that these crouched, thin-legged scavengers were extraordinarily ugly relatives of the cats – he would have taken them for ordinary mutts. The way they wrestled for the last remains of a carcass, always at each other's throats, had nothing to do with proud toms. Only an aberration of evolution, could have assigned these unspeakable creatures to the cat branch of the animals' pedigree. Vertebrates, clearly. Mammals, natural. But cats? He thought that these shaggy, bone-sucking good-for-nothings should rather trade as rodents. Even better as dogs, since they spend their lives just as cowardly in packs and are generally unkempt. With their remarkably small heads, the blurred fur-stains and the steeply sloping flanks, they were hardly to look at. Literally unsightly. "Their small brains probably don't allow any more sophisticated hunt-strategies than to scrape others' leftovers together. Only the vultures are worse than those dumpster divers," he thought to himself. It was running down his back in freezing cold and he shook himself once from head to tail.

"Stupid hyenas!" he muttered and paused for a while. "They're fake, those would-be lions!" he then quietly meowed to himself, "Ugly both inside and out. Worst ever." He was happy when the hyena scenes were alternated with landscapes.

The whole evening he watched attentively the film about the animal world of the African savannah and meowed like a football commentator. Except that he was not following a sporting competition of equal athletes, but the harsh reality of real life in the wild. It was not fair play, but rather the law of the jungle that ordered the coexistence of the animals. The survival of the fittest was the standard and premise of all actions. The dramatic divergence of fates at the top and bottom of the food chain crystallized in the sight of triumphant winners feeding on the mangled losers. Only a few were able to muddle through like the hyenas. Mostly, however, the redemption of one had to be bought by an equal tribute from the other. Hunter and prey could not both be satisfied. This principle of wilderness corresponded to his view of the world and he thought to himself, "Unfortunately the earth is no wonderland. It is extremely rough. You have to fight for everything – you eat, or get eaten. And losers will always be losers. It's as simple as that."

The television program was entirely to his taste and he experienced an evening of educational and at the same time varied entertainment that was rarely seen before. No dating show, no quiz and certainly no made-up superheroes. No, there were real superheroes to admire!

He loved to lounge around watching TV and make a comment every now and then. "They're the best! Nobody beats them," he meowed at the sight of lions and "Sneaky jackals!" when hyenas were shown again. "Delusional creatures!" he meowed and "Sad!"

The longer the animal film ran, the calmer he became. Long shots, extensive landscapes and the soft voice of the speaker made him gradually tired. He yawned more and more often with his mouth wide open, bending the tip of his tongue upwards. His eyelids became heavier and heavier, the blinking slowed down visibly. He had to lie down more comfortably and his heckling became slower and less frequent. "Failing hyenas," he murmured softly, "born stupid." Again and again he fell asleep for seconds and was only awakened by his head slumping away. The futile jumping of a wild dog after a gerbil, who disappeared in wind-speed in a hole, still elicited a "Fool!" from him before his head fell to the side again. The futile sprint of a lion behind a successfully escaped gazelle, he commented with "Hoax!" before his eyes closed again briefly.

The family watched the spectacle attentively and whispered after each of the cat's meows. They were fascinated by how their pet dealt with the events on the television and made his opinion known. Whispering wildly, each meow was discussed controversially until the next meow sparked a new discussion and made the last one forgotten. The opinions diverged.

The more often the tomcat drifted off into the realm of dreams, the more incomprehensible his utterances became, until he finally meowed a barely understandable phrase, with his head resting firmly on his paws with his eyes closed.

"What did he say?" asked the mother in a whisper at room volume.

"I have no idea," said the son.

The father shrugged his shoulders.

"I think he mewed 'fev-something'," said the daughter.

"Excuse me?" said the mother, "fev-what?" the father.

"Fevcoco, I believe?" said the daughter tentatively. "I don't know what that means."

"Fevcoco? That's garbage!" said the mother.

"He must have meant something," said the son.

"And what do you think it means?" asked the mother curtly.

"I don't know, maybe it's a riddle!" said the son.

"Have fun solving it! You love this guy, but 'fevcoco' is totally gaga," replied the mother.

The father interrupted the budding argument. "Guys! Look! He is sleeping. He probably meowed that when he fell asleep. That's why it makes no sense."

"Even when he's awake, his meows often don't make sense!" With this, the mother ended the topic and took a quieter tone. "But as long as he's sleeping, we should talk about what to do with him."

"What are you talking about, mom?" The son asked reproachfully. "What do you want to do with him?"

"At least not what we've been doing so far," she replied.

"What then, Mom?" asked the daughter.

"Don't act so stupid! The tomcat has become unbearable. We just sneak around him carefully so as not to annoy him," said the mother.

"Maybe you!" said the son.

"That's right, I still think he's the best," said the daughter.

"Until he scratches you! That's getting too touchy for me. He is stronger than any of us now," said the mother forcefully.

"His strength is what's great about him," the son objected. "He is just no well-behaved pussycat. The whole street respects him!"

"Pssst," hissed the mother. "Anyway, the fact is that he's not as cute and sweet as he was in the beginning. He is dangerous. And he's getting increasingly brazen."

"He just wants to be spoiled. Like everybody! You too," said the daughter with folded arms.

"You've seen what can happen when he gets angry. His mood changes very quickly and then you are on the hit list. What if he attacks one of us? We won't stand a chance," said the mother and looked over at her husband. "You say something too! The cat should listen to us – not the other way around!"

"A cat is not a dog, darling!"

"But that's not a normal cat anymore. He's huge and he's growing. If that doesn't scare you, that's good for you."

"Mom, you're going totally overboard! You just don't like him because he snarled at you. But that was normal – you totally snubbed him," said the son.

"Exactly," said the daughter, "if you annoy him, it is clear that he will defend himself. We never had problems with him before. But we don't do anything to him either. That's why he likes us."

"Are you guys lost?" The mother was stunned. "What do you think will happen to you if he changes his mind?"

"Why should he do that? We are in his team. You really have no idea!" The son shook his head.

"Hey! Not in that tone," the father admonished him.

"Thanks!" said the mother to her husband and turned back to the children. "Maybe this is what he wants. For us to fight."

"What would he get out of that, mom?" asked the daughter.

"If we don't stick together, he has a free rein. Then we are busy with ourselves and can't put up a fight."

"And what do you suggest we do, dear?" asked the father.

"Maybe we should start to put him in his place. For example, we could forbid him to go to the fence and hiss at the neighbor's dog. Or we could forbid him to lie down in our beds. And if he doesn't do what we want, we'll tell him to go to hell," suggested the mother.

Daughter and son looked at each other with open mouths. "Go to hell? We'll see about that," said the son. "Exactly! We gotta decide that together," cried the daughter.

"Do you have a better idea?" the father asked calmly.

"Unlike you, we don't want to punish him," the daughter answered and turned to her mother, "but if you want to prevent him from getting mad at you again, we could give him his own room."

"Good idea! As far as I know, the study is not used very often," said the son with a broad grin.

The mother's facial features were slipping away. "Oh, great. That's quite the opposite of what I want! Do you want to reward the cat for his behavior? Then he'll certainly behave better in the future. Good idea!"

With a gentle touch on her forearm, the father tried to calm his wife down. "Maybe it's not such a bad idea." The mother raised her eyebrows expectantly before the father continued: "Look, you've been complaining that he is spreading himself too much. If we expand his area a little bit, you could get out of each other's way for now."

"You said it: *for now*. After a short time, he's gotten used to it and is worse than before." The mother waved them off. "This is exactly the wrong thing to do."

"I think it's worth a try. What do you think, children?"

Wordlessly, both raised their hands to testify their agreement.

Rocking his head from side to side, the father also raised his hand to vote and looked hesitantly at the mother. Horrified, she cried, "Darling, what is this?"

"Motion accepted!" cried the son.

"Passed!" added the daughter and pointed her finger at her mother. "Ha!"

"Waaaaait a second!" she replied. Accusingly, she looked at her husband and said, "We must first agree before we can vote here."

"This isn't fair!" cried the daughter.

"We have decided!" cried the son. "And you lost!"

Father and mother looked deep into each other's eyes. You could see them struggling inside. Finally, the father said, "I'll allow it."

The mother was furious. "I beg your pardon?"

"Innocent until proven guilty," he countered dryly.

"Proven guilty? That's too late!"

"Well, mom, he gets his own room!" the children cheered.

The father warned them to be quiet. "Not so loud. The cat is asleep!"

The son leaned provocatively over the table to the parents and whispered so quietly that they had to lean against him if they wanted to understand him. "We can vote on whether we introduce the following rule: Anyone who speaks disparagingly about him again behind his back will be reported."

"That is nonsense! We have voted and decided. But now it is enough! Off to bed with you, it's late," the father ended the discussion.

The children ran happily to the second floor and went to bed quickly. The parents sat next to each other for a while and watched the still sleeping cat in front of the TV.

Finally, the mother said, "It was wrong to reward the cat for his aggression. Could cost us dearly."

"We decided together as a family," the father said.

"After all," replied the mother.

"What do you mean by that?"

"After all, we're still the ones who decide."

21 – I'm in no hurry

Someone had turned off the TV while he was sleeping. He had a nightmare that had been so real that the tomcat would not be able to shake it all day long:

He had been back with Monty and the many colorful flowers in the garden were ready to be sniffed. As always, the house was in need of renovation, yet it seemed inviting. The family had also been yakking loudly, as he was used to.

But something distinguished this dream from reality. Nobody, enthused by Monty's meows, gathered the whole family together. They understood him, but had not followed any of his instructions. Amused, they even commented on Monty's wish for a fresh crate. "You want a fresh crate? Then get yourself one! Why are these silly cats so crazy about cardboard boxes, anyway?" Monty seemed helpless, was much smaller than in reality and degenerated into a caricature of himself. A joke made of flesh and fur. It was unimaginable to admire this cat.

In this nightmare, the orange tomcat was degraded to an onlooker and – like watching an animal film – not able to intervene. And instead of savannah kings, he saw in his mind's eye a tomcat who was no longer master of the situation. There was nothing to suggest that Monty was the head of the family. The dream became worse from minute to minute. The family laughed at Monty and chased him around until he finally ran away and disappeared into a hiding place in the farthest corner of the property. He fearfully crouched under a bush and grew smaller and smaller. Shrunk to a kitten.

Suddenly Monty was hanging upside down, his front legs dangling down and his face bloated and covered in blood. The dead tomcat peeled open his empty eyes once more and urgently stared at his orange friend. With the flickering voice of late realization, Monty whispered, "Everyone dies according to their character," before the final tension was released from his body.

Horror shot through the orange cat's limbs and made him wake from his nightmare. The living room was dark and quiet when he opened his eyes with sweaty paws. His orange fur was pressed so tightly to his body that it trembled. His ears were burning hot. Seeing Monty like that was horrible. The image of the friend dangling from a railing – deprived of all authority and dignity – haunted him. The day had just begun and was already ruined. Not even the hunger that usually set in after awakening built up.

His open eyes gazed unfocused into nothingness while he thought about his dream for quite a while. But no matter how he twisted and turned it around, he couldn't make out a deeper meaning in the story. Yet, like many tomcats before him, he was merely blinded by his own self-confidence. His premonition, of which he was so sure, failed.

Nothing helped. So, he decided to get up and stomp around the house to see what was going on. The dream followed him and his mood was very bad. If somebody would cross him today, he could not guarantee anything. He suspiciously crept around every corner and slowly put one paw in front of the other. Deep breaths moved the air through his teeth pressed tightly together.

"The house is suspiciously quiet. Where is everyone?" he thought, searching the first floor. In the kitchen, he found the mother standing in front of open cupboards and drawers, assessing the food supplies. She seemed lost in thought, and even the usually loud squawking radio was silent. On quiet paws, he approached the mother, who only noticed him when she turned around and he stood only a few inches away from her. Reflexively, she tore her hands protectively before her. A packet of salt slipped from her fingers and fell to the ground.

"You scared me to death! Don't sneak up on me like that," she called out. She had to gather herself for a moment and then bent down for the package. "Phew, luckily it didn't split open. That would have been a huge mess."

He thought to himself, "Has this nut job really forgotten the mess I left on the carpet? *That* was huge!" But he said nothing. Instead, he looked at her silently and waited for a reaction.

"Go upstairs. There's a surprise for you," she finally said, probably to get rid of him.

"Great!" he muttered and turned around. He left the mother behind to go upstairs and see what it was all about.

When he arrived at the landing, he already heard a rumbling and rustling from the study. He slowly went through the door and took a careful look into the room. The daughter noticed him immediately and called out, "There you are! Come in. This is all yours from now on. The study is hardly used anyway. Look! You can lie down here." She patted with her flat hand on a thick, soft blanket that she had draped on an old sofa bed that was actually kept ready for overnight guests. "The blanket is as fluffy as you are. Well, do you like it?"

"Classy," he meowed and nodded appreciatively. She grinned as if she had heard him speak for the first time.

He was flattered to be given his own room, even though the change of use did not mean a great loss for the family. There was very little work there and overnight guests were rare. It was rather a storage room for unused furniture. Nevertheless, he wondered why he was given his own room, and why now of all times. He wondered, because just like there is no round rectangle, there is no gift without a reason.

"Why?" he meowed.

"We decided this last night in the family powwow when you were asleep. You should relax a little and feel good. We'll take out the desk and you can also get a TV if you like. We know how much you love to watch TV," the daughter explained.

Taking slow steps, he climbed on the sofa and tested its elasticity by alternately dipping his front paws into it a couple of times. His claws clung to the blanket and lifted it with every tug. "Terrific sofa," he meowed. "Tremendously soft."

The daughter smiled broadly and jumped up to him on the sofa to cuddle him. "I'm glad you like it." She gave him a kiss on the forehead and ran out.

He looked after her suspiciously. He did not trust them. Why did they decide behind his back that he should have his own room? What was the purpose of this secret arrangement? "Why such collusion?" he thought to himself. "If anyone is colluding, it's me!"

He sat on his new sofa and let time pass. But he couldn't relax, couldn't let the matter rest. The thought that his family could try to manipulate him, or even hatch a plan against him, could not be dismissed. Should he be made obedient? He brooded. "They probably think they can bribe me with a room. But I actually own the whole house anyway. And the garden to boot."

Were they going to move him to the secluded room to have more space for themselves? Did the family want to test him? And if so, for what? Did they want to distract from something? Maybe, but from what? Or were these thoughts exaggerated and they really just wanted to reward him because they loved him so much? Possibly, because after all he was sure of the affection of the children. But he had doubts about the parents. Of course the mother didn't like him, but what could she do?

"Why this gift? Why now?" he asked himself. Whatever the family was up to, it couldn't hurt to get to the bottom of it and get his family back in line if necessary. And so he left the seclusion of his new home and went back to the first floor to see what was going on.

There everything was normal. Suspiciously normal. The mother was still busy in the kitchen, the daughter was on the phone with God knows who and the son was lying in front of the TV. Through the open garden door, he saw the father mowing the lawn, which, in addition to the wonderful smell of freshly cut grass, also made an outrageous noise.

He passed those who stayed inside and went outside. Everything seemed normal. Even the neighbor's dog was annoying as usual and barked at the relentless roar of the mower. "How can you get so upset about everything?" the cat thought. "Why this eternal noise?"

The dog ran barking along the fence and always stayed even with the father, who slowly pushed the lawnmower in front of him. "Get lost, you stupid mutt!" he shouted. But it was useless, because the angry dog followed the man wherever he went. Droning, barking, screaming. Obviously annoyed, the neighbor came running in quick steps from his terrace to the property line. "Is this necessary? It's the weekend! We're trying to have breakfast in peace," he shouted to the father, trying to channel the sound by holding his hands to the corners of his mouth like a funnel.

The father tried to remain calm, although he had to shout to be heard. "I'll be done soon. The lawn isn't that big."

The neighbor did not let this calm him. "Will you hurry up?"

"It would be quieter if the dog wouldn't bark so much," the father called back.

"What nerve! He's only barking because you're making such a racket!"

"I can't hear you! It's too loud," replied the father, turned away and grinned with pleasure.

The neighbor got angry and began to yell until his head turned red. The father stoically continued mowing and pretended not to hear anything. For a few yards the neighbor ran after the father as before his own dog and gesticulated wildly. Finally, the father turned off the mower and got into the argument, in the course of which even the oldest animosities were taken out of the moth box. From the smoke and smell of barbecue in summer to autumn leaves on the wrong side of the fence. The to and fro of the ever more loudly produced arguments and pseudo-arguments gradually called all members of both families to the scene. Even without a lawnmower, the volume reached ever greater proportions, so that all around, people looked out of their windows with concern.

The spectacle amused the cat who watched from the terrace. He was quite entertained by the people bickering like children. Although it hardly seemed necessary, he perhaps wanted to add a little momentum to the whole thing. Because a proper row between the families would be undoubtedly good for him. One could stir up the mangy dog owners next door and his family's attention was drawn away from him for a while – just until he could figure out what was going on. Silently, he approached and took up a stance behind his people.

The dog lived out its innate protective instinct and jumped up at the fence barking incessantly. The claws furrowed the wood and the teeth flashed out briefly each time he stretched his face over the slats. The tomcat found this hopping and nagging as pathetic as the fact that it probably filled its owner with pride.

"Don't come any closer or you'll get bitten," the neighbor shouted to the father.

"Call off your dog," he replied.

Before everyone could start talking at the same time, the cat chimed in with a short and loud hiss. The people fell silent and looked at him. Without any movement, he looked at the neighbors through the fence and meowed quietly, "We need a higher fence!"

"Yes, we are building the best fence in the world," cried the son. "Then we won't have to put up with you anymore!"

"As if that would help! The fence won't keep out noise or anything else, you fool!" replied the neighbor.

"Wrong," meowed the cat. "Fences work."

"This cat is really the very worst. Maybe this stupid, arrogant creature needs a shower again," cried the neighbor.

Then the son freaked out. "If you do that again, there'll be real trouble!"

"He'd deserve it! Lying around and mewing nasty stuff. We'd be ashamed to have such an unworthy pet!"

"I'll be right over," cried the son and held his clenched fist against the neighbor.

"I'm sure you won't go over!" cried the mother.

With his hands up, the father tried to calm the situation down. "Now let's all take it down a notch! Perhaps it would be best if everyone took care of their own problems."

"But they are our problem!" cried the son and pointed to the neighbors.

"You're going in now!" ordered the mother.

The cat also tried to calm the waters. "Come on, let's go," he meowed toward the son. "They're a complete and total joke."

"OK," said the son through his clenched teeth, "but this is not over yet. Next time I'll kick his ass!"

"Hey! I heard that, you rascal!" the neighbor still shouted, but the two turned around and slowly walked back to the house side by side.

"Just stay calm!" he meowed to the son, "We'll hit them 1,000 times harder than they hit us."

On his way through the living room and up the stairs, the son scolded the neighbor with wild gestures. The cat followed him with slow steps and listened calmly. Arriving in his room, the son sat down on the bed, paused briefly and said, "If he turns on you again or splashes you wet, there will be revenge." With eyes wide open, he waited for a reaction from the cat.

He remained silent for a moment and rotated once or twice before lying down. Finally, he lifted his head and returned the son's deep gaze. "They are not after me. They are after you."

"What? Why?"

"They think they're better than us. They go at me to get at you," he meowed.

"What should I do?" son asked then.

"Get rid of them – these rodent-infested haters," he meowed.

"I will! I can start anytime! You just have to say so." The son seemed determined to do everything.

"I'm in no hurry with the neighbors," he meowed and looked briefly at the door to make sure no one was listening. "Just stand by. Your day to be courageous will come."

"OK!" said the son hesitantly. "I hope I'll have the courage then!"

"Believe me, my boy, you will! You will be a lion, not a sheep."

"Um-hum," replied the son.

Confidently, the cat nodded slowly and winked.

Then he got up, left the son in his room and went downstairs to the first floor. From the living room window, the cat watched the scenery at the property line. The heated discussion between the parents on one side and the neighbors on the other side had gradually cooled down. Especially the appeasing gestures and conciliatory nature of the mother were able to prevent worse from happening. Nevertheless, the cat was satisfied, so a smile flashed across his face. Without much action, there had been a skirmish that could not have gotten out of hand any faster. At the same time, he was able to present himself as a levelheaded mediator. Fantastic.

From behind, the hamster Jonny interrupted the cat's world of thoughts. "Quite satisfied?" he shouted in animal language.

"Oh, I forgot that you are still sitting in your little cage," the cat answered smugly. "But yes, I am quite content."

"You have just shown your best side. Pious and intent on peace."

"Am I not?" he asked slowly and raised an eyebrow.

"You can't pretend to be anything to anyone. Everyone knows that you hate the neighbors, especially the dog."

"I'm the least hateful cat there is."

"Lie!" cried Jonny. "Another lie!"

"What do you think the truth is?"

"You are hateful and need the fighting. It's just a pity that the mother is settling your lovely squabble! You will be on the hit list very soon," cried the hamster.

"You are wrong, once again. What you see here is the calm before the storm. The tensions are shifted into the future time and time again, accumulate and then break out all the more violently." The tomcat paused briefly. "Look: With her soothing hand movements the mother reminds me of the Nordic king Cnut the Great. According to legend, he had his throne set up on the beach and tried to tame the tide. Just like him, the mother will also fail."

Jonny's empty eyes revealed his fear that the cat could be right.

22 – They're weak

His fur reflected the low sun in copper tones. It rose and fell with every breath he took. He sat at the window and looked contentedly at the hustle and bustle in the garden, whose opposite he seemed to embody. He blinked slowly while the people hurriedly presented their arguments, tracing them with their hands in the air.

Jonny also watched, standing on his hind legs and holding on to the crossbars of the grating with his small hamster hands. To see a little more, he made himself very long until he almost fell over. The rodent was usually running around in his cage, but now completely calm and seemed thoughtful. Instead of the otherwise usual wild calls: Concentration.

The previously exchanged thoughts had an effect. Wordlessly, the two observed how the neighborhood fight gradually settled under the moderating influence of the mother. The gestures became more conciliatory and the first people went back to their homes.

Finally, Jonny broke the silence. "Do you see? Everyone goes home, nothing happened. Your plan is not working."

"What plan?" asked the cat.

"Well, the thing about the calm before the storm. What about your storm?"

"Wait," muttered the cat.

"Look, the matter is settled. No quarreling and no fighting."

"The calm before the storm has only just begun! You just have to wait and see."

"It's terrible how you look forward to a fight. If our family broke apart over it, you wouldn't care!"

As one might expect, the cat had a more favorable opinion about his intentions. "Au contraire, you half a portion of a half portion. What you don't understand with your hamster brain is that I want to make this family one! A conflict is exactly what this family needs to get back together."

"You don't need to fight with other people to strengthen togetherness," cried the hamster.

"Only in contrast to the stranger does what is shared become clear," said the cat dryly.

"Aren't you laying it on a little thick?"

The cat slowly turned his gaze away from the garden and looked at the hamster urgently. "Doesn't this degenerate world need a little pathos?"

"At least it doesn't need sociopaths and provocateurs like you! We should rather work together with our neighbors. To understand each other. Then everyone would feel better."

"It's not about being well. When people are doing well, they become comfortable and question the circumstances. And those who question the circumstances divide more than they unite."

The hamster shook his head in disbelief. "So you don't want our family to be glad?"

"You don't want to understand me, do you? To be happy, a community needs a cleansing, a renewal from time to time. It needs to reassure itself anew. And to recognize itself, a quarrel with a stranger is always better than a quarrel within. You will agree with me there!"

"By no means! In the end, it is all about creating a balance over and over again. For that you can simply talk. It's exhausting and takes time, but at some point you reach an agreement. That's a healthy argument," Jonny said imploringly.

"Or you talk and talk and talk and at some point you can't reach an agreement at all. Discussions are tiring and usually end in frustration," he said, not sounding as if he still wanted to be persuaded.

"I'm sure people will realize in time what you're up to and tell you to go to hell. Surely everything will turn out for the good!"

"You're just like the humans, dear Johnny."

"What do you mean?" asked the hamster astonished.

The cat turned away and looked through the window into the distance. "Oh, you know, people always fall back to the hope that history will turn out in their favor. But history has refuted this good faith countless times. People are naive. And they're weak." A couple of seconds passed until he continued. "We're gonna have to see what happens."

Without saying anything back, the hamster stared anxiously out the window. The deep purring, which is characteristic of satisfied cats, filled the room.

Nearly a lion

He had come a long way. So far that he was even rewarded for urinating on the carpet. What else could he bring this family to? It could be manipulated and divided. Their unconditional obedience and inability to stand up to him caused contempt to sprout in him.

Like a lion enthroned above everything, a feeling of total authority filled him – and it made him grow. Until he himself was almost as big and powerful as a lion. There wasn't far to go.

23 – Total fool

Uneventful days passed. It was hot. People and animals moved even less than the air, which was only kept moving by fans and its own flickering above the asphalt. The trees craved water and even the withered grass no longer protected his paws from the ever-hotter ground. Condemned to doing nothing, one could only watch how everything and everyone got warmer and warmer.

But the atmosphere is like a kettle on the stove. The temperature does not rise incessantly. At some point, the energy supplied discharges as steam through the boiler whistle. And so, after long days of temperature stagnation, far away a roll of thunder announced the inevitable release.

Dark clouds approached quickly. A thunderstorm was imminent. A clearly refreshing wind provided cooling and mobilized the tired limbs. The family was startled, running and talking in disarray. The sudden change in the weather made them close the doors and windows. Outside, there was a need to quickly tidy up what needed to be sorted before wind and rain would derange and destroy it all. On both sides of the fence, people wanted their belongings weatherproof. In the face of the storm, it was up to every family to help themselves – to put themselves first.

Quickly, the father passed his daughter, who hectically cleared the garden table, and called out to her. "Could you go upstairs right away and look after the skylights? And tell your brother to come help!"

"Yes," she answered with bottles under her arms and too many glasses in her hands. "But I'm going to take this into the kitchen quick."

"Okay, I'll go out front and put all the odds and ends in the garage."

"Don't forget to bring in the garbage can, dear," cried the mother while closing the windows in the living room. "All the crap got spread out in the front yard during the last storm!"

"That's exactly what I intend to do!" replied the father tersely.

The son took two steps at once running down the stairs and fell into the backyard. "What should I do, Dad?" he shouted after his father.

"Clear away the garden furniture," he replied before he disappeared around the corner.

"OK," the son shouted into the wind and set to work.

The family's restlessness seemed to be transferred to Jonny the hamster, as he bounced his head up and down while still clinging to the cage. He shook the bars violently, but the clattering was enveloped in the general hubbub and no one paid any attention to him. The loud squeaking of his high voice fell on deaf ears. It was a whistling in the wind. No one listened to him.

The cat watched the general bustle with great amusement. "They are more afraid of the rain than I am," he thought and smiled a little. Demonstratively calm, he strolled after the son outside, where the wind blew into his fur and exposed his pale white scalp. It looked cute, but he did not let anything show. He sat down at the end of the terrace and watched the son carry two chairs with big steps towards the small garden shed on the other end of the property.

At the same time, the dog ran around the neighbor's yard aimlessly and nervously, barking at everyone who crossed his path. He even tried to bite into the wind and attached himself to the calves and knees of people running around. The neighbor almost stumbled over the dog when he suddenly stood in front of his shin. With a loud scream and a gentle kick, he shooed the animal out of his way.

"Typical mutt," thought the tomcat, "this overrated flea circus is not even good at staying out of the way! But when mommy says 'sit', he'll sit!"

Meanwhile, the wind was getting stronger and stronger. A gust hit the seating group on the neighbor's terrace and went under the tabletop like under the wing of a starting airplane. And just as slowly, the heavy wooden table detached itself from the floor. It hovered just above the ground for several yards until one of the table legs rammed into the lawn. The round table toppled over, but instead of lying upside down, it rolled over the grass like a tumbleweed through the desert.

The disaster took its course. As if in slow motion, the huge disk inevitably raced towards the fence. Faster and faster, until it finally struck with a loud bang. Bursting wood cracked and groaned. The demarcation line, which until then had given the neighborhood dispute a clearly defined border, was torn. Fragments flew through the air like shrapnel, barely missing the son walking directly next to it.

"Hey," the son shouted at the neighbor and flinched. Only one step separated him from the place where the remains of the table and fence lay wedged together. "What was that? Watch out!"

The neighbor ran in big steps to the accident site. "Are you okay?" he shouted to the son. But his gaze revealed that he was more concerned about the damage to his property.

"No, but it almost hit me! Damn it!"

"Calm down! Nothing happened to you," cried the neighbor when he arrived on the scene.

The ball of wood made of table and fence remains swayed in the wind like a boat lying at anchor. Again and again small splinters flew in the direction of the son, who stretched out his hands in front of him for protection. "You can see that all this is about to blow up in our faces. Give me a hand," he called out to the neighbor and tried in vain to push the fence back into an upright position.

"Move aside," said the neighbor, reached over the fence and pushed the son aside. "The table is too heavy! This is not going to work. I'll do it!" He tried to pull the table out of the fence and grabbed its remnants. He had to pull hard and a splinter bored itself into his hand. "Ahhhh! Damn it!"

The cry of pain called out the dog. Snarling mingled with the sounds of the storm. Grrrrr! With front paws broad and pressed firmly into the ground, the dog kept his head ducked and stared at the son. Taking small steps, the dog groped closer and closer.

"Hold your mutt back!" cried the son.

The neighbor held his hand and, with a painfully distorted face, squeezed a few drops of blood between his fingers. "Are you afraid?"

"Just hold him back! He thinks I've hurt you!"

"Damn! Calm down! He won't do anything," the neighbor yelled at the son without looking up from his hand.

The dog growled. "There'll be real trouble if he bites me," cried the son, grabbed a severed table leg and held it in front of him like a sword.

The cat did not want to miss the event and came closer. His orange mane blew like a thousand little flags as he set up near the fence. Through narrow eye slits, he aimed at the dog, which he clearly surpassed in height. The dog began to bark nervously, crawling ever closer to the fence lying on the ground. After one more step the dog stood on the fence, which swayed under him like a trampoline. He barked incessantly and came so close that the son reflexively took a step back and with his table leg split the air in front of the dog's nose. Rip, rip, rip, as if he was playing tennis without a ball.

"Stop it! You're provoking him. Can't you see that, you maniac?" cried the neighbor.

"He's going to bite me!" cried the son.

"That's on you then!"

The son looked at the cat for help. "Don't be afraid of it," he meowed, looking him straight in the eyes. "He's a total fool."

Then the son turned around and forcefully threw the table leg in the direction of the dog. Hit in the nose, he howled so loudly it would chill anyone to the bone. Confused by this hard blow, the dog staggered back into his own garden.

"Heeey!" cried the neighbor. "What was that, you miserable bastard?" He seemed to have forgotten the pain in his hand and climbed between the wooden fragments. Obviously, he wanted to get at the throat of the son, who, robbed of his weapon, looked anxiously at the cat, as if he wanted to ask him what to do.

"Don't take it," the cat meowed. "Be brutal, be tough!"

The son nodded, his lips pressed together. As he turned around, he swung out and punched the neighbor standing on the shaky fence remnant against his chest. With a deep sigh, the victim sank to his knees, holding his chest with one hand and the wobbly ground underneath him with the other. He had to collect himself for a moment before he stood up without a word and gave the son a blow. He pushed and shoved back. A scuffle ensued, within seconds the fists flew.

Without interfering, the tomcat watched the scene and let the two opponents decide who was stronger. He would not put his thumb on this scale.

Long seconds passed until a creaking sound broke through the rumbling. The son collapsed. A groan preceded the muffled bang of the skull hitting the ground.

24 – Not good

The son lay on his stomach. Twisted and motionless, as if sleeping. The blood running from his ear made them fear the worst. The neighbor had quickly disappeared from the scene after the young man had gone down. The debris at the property line, which had just been fought over, receded into irrelevance.

Right next to the son sat the cat. Although neither blood nor dirt adhered to his paws, he felt the urge to wash them thoroughly. Calmly as on any other day, he licked them off, but more conscientiously. They should be pure, not just clean.

The constantly whistling wind prevented him from noticing how the mother approached from behind. She pressed her lips firmly together until her mouth was only a couple of inches wide. The eyebrows almost touched in rage.

"What happened here?" she cried.

The tomcat turned around, pretended to be completely uninvolved and meowed, "I got it very much under control!"

"What have you done?" the mother yelled at the cat.

"Nothing! It was that clown next door. He's out of control!"

"No! It was you! You talked him into this! What did you say to my child?" she screamed at the cat.

"I don't want anyone dying," he meowed.

"WHAT DID YOU SAY TO HIM?"

"What I said was perfect," he meowed calmly, shrugged his shoulders and turned the inside of his paws up.

"Nonsense! You instigated him! It was you!"

"I'll fix it," he meowed calmly.

Despair mingled with the mother's gaze. Tears filled her eyes. The sight of her son lying on the ground seemed to have fallen into her heart like lead. She shook her head, holding her hands in front of her mouth.

"No," she whispered to herself. "No, I'll fix it myself."

As if out of nowhere, she pulled out a pistol and aimed at the lion-sized tomcat, who could hardly be missed from this short distance. Her hand was shaking, her knuckles were white. It was unclear whether she was holding the gun, or whether she was holding onto it. But her determination gave the cat a very rare feeling: fear. His fur instantly lost the copper shine. It was just dull and lusterless and seemed almost unreal.

As if surprised by a Marian apparition, he looked at the mother. Frozen like a stone still breathing. He was only able to meow a shy, "Not good!" Bent and deprived of all dynamism, he seemed a little smaller right away. "Do I get no credit for ...?"

"ENOUGH OF THIS CRAP! Enough of this damn nonsense meowing, you fat cat!"

She squeezed the trigger and her eyes shut. Bam, bam, bam. One bullet after the other flew out of the barrel until it clicked. Slowly she opened her eyes again. First one, then the other. Suddenly the storm had died down. The gun smoke forced her to blink. It was difficult to focus anything through the cloud. Only very gradually the air cleared. She rubbed her watery eyes. The bang of the gun had left a shrill beeping in her ears that drowned out the dead silence surrounding her. Her senses were foggy.

Nervously she tried to find the cat, afraid she had missed him. But in front of her she saw: nothing. No blood, no pieces of fur lying around, no carcass. Nothing. Even behind her back: Nothing. Incredulous, she turned around several times in all directions and slowly took two steps back. Had the tomcat been wounded and rescued himself into a bush and lay there helplessly? Had he escaped at the last second and was just sneaking around her unnoticed, ready to fight back? Again she looked over her shoulders. But she couldn't see him anywhere, couldn't hear him.

Hands trembling, she held the empty weapon in front of her and took another step back. And there she suddenly saw a small, well-behaved, orange cat right in front of her feet. Was that him?

A normal house cat like all the others, not a lion and not a lynx. Unharmed. Innocent. He opened his mouth, but not a word came out between his teeth, just a soft, sweet hissing that would not have frightened a mouse.

"What's going on here?" murmured the mother. "Is that you?"

The little cat looked up at her in confusion. *Meow.*

Dumbfounded, the mother paused for a moment, brows furrowed. Finally, she shouted at the little animal: "GET LOST!"

Then he winced, jumped up and ran away. With his narrow shoulders and hips he fitted exactly between two fence slats. He ran until he could no longer be seen, until he merged with the grey of the distant landscape.

When the mother turned back to her son, he slowly opened his eyes, held his head and stammered softly, "Where is he?"

For a few seconds she looked into the distance where she had last seen the cat. "He's gone. Blown away. Never to return."

please rate and review this book

Tremendous help! Huge thanks!